The United States

使用英語的國家

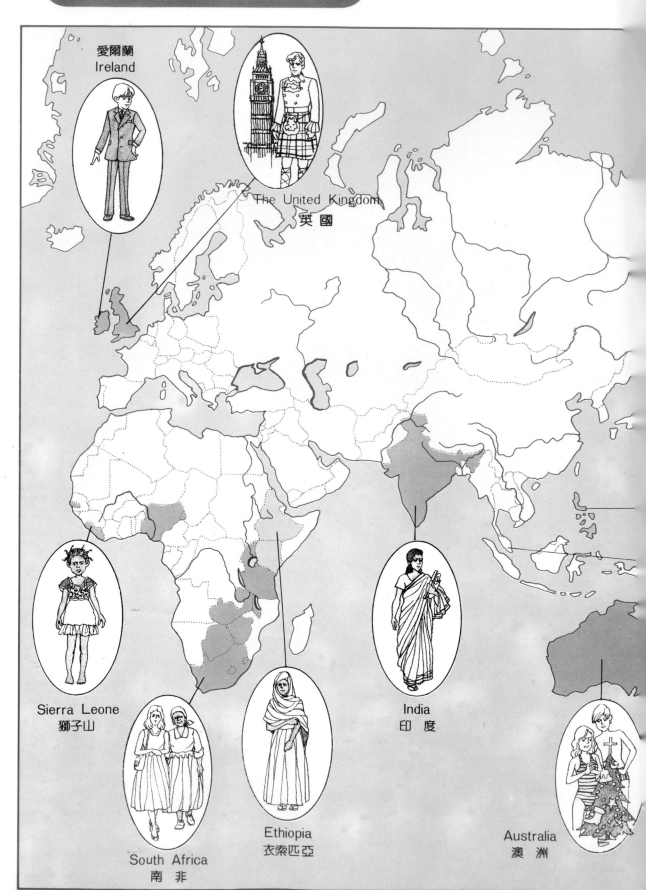

愛爾蘭
Ireland

The United Kingdom
英國

Sierra Leone
獅子山

South Africa
南非

Ethiopia
衣索匹亞

India
印度

Australia
澳洲

Canada
加拿大

Philippines
菲律賓

Singapore
新加坡

The United States of America
美　國

Guyana
蓋亞那

New Zealand
紐西蘭

The United Kingdom

LEARNER'S
AMERICAN TALKS
2

LEARNING PUBLISHING CO., LTD.

Editorial Staff

- ●企劃・編著 / 陳怡平
- ●英文撰稿
  Mark A. Pengra ・ David Bell
  Edward C. Yulo ・ John C. Didier
- ●校訂
  劉　毅・葉淑霞・陳威如・王慶銘・王怡華
  林順隆・林佩汀・陳瑠琍・喻小敏・項福瑩
  梁艾琳・王慧芬・黃正齡・鄭淳文・蕭錦玲
- ●校閱
  Larry J. Marx ・ Lois M. Findler
  John H. Voelker ・ Keith Gaunt
- ●封面設計 / 張鳳儀
- ●插畫 / 林惠貞
- ●版面設計 / 張鳳儀・林惠貞
- ●版面構成 / 蘇淑玲
- ●打字
  黃淑貞・倪秀梅・吳秋香・徐湘君

CONTENTS

AMERICAN TALKS

PRINT IN TAIWAN

supervisor   :   Samuel Liu
text design   :   Jessica Y.P. Chen
illustrations :   Isabella Chang, Jennifer Lin, Sherling Sue
cover design :   Isabella Chang

ACKNOWLEDGEMENTS

We would like to thank all the people whose ongoing support has made this project so enjoyable and rewarding. At the top of the list of those who provided insight, inspiration, and helpful suggestions for revisions are:

David Bell
Mark A. Pengra
Rebecca S.H. Yeh
Michelle Chen
Melody Wang
Clement Wang
Stella Yu
Marge Chen
Irene Liang
Jesmine Hwang
Sabrina Wang
Winifred Jeng
Bessie Hsiang
Pei-ting Lin

序 言

　　編者在受教育的過程中，常覺國內的英語教育，欠缺一套好的會話教材。根據我們最近所做的研究顯示，各級學校的英語老師與關心的讀者也都深深覺得，我們用的進口會話教材，版面密密麻麻，不但引不起學習興趣，所學又不盡與實際生活相關。像一般會話書上所教的早餐，總是教外國人吃的 *cereal*（麥片粥），而完全沒有提及中國人早餐吃的稀飯（香港餐館一般翻成 " *congee* "，美國人叫它 " *rice soup* "）、豆漿（ *soy bean milk* ）、燒餅（ *baked roll* ）、油條（*Chinese frit-ter* ）該如何適切地表達？

　　我們有感於一套好的教材必須能夠真正引發學生的興趣，內容要切合此時此地（ *here and now* ）及讀者確實的需求，也就是要本土化、具體化。

　　兩年多來，在這種共識之下，我們全體編輯群秉持專業化的精神，實地蒐集、調查日常生活中天天用得到、聽得到的會話，加以歸類、整理，並設計生動有趣的教學活動，彙編成 " *AMERICAN TALKS* "這套最適合中國人的英語會話教材。

　　這套教材不僅在資料蒐集上力求完美，而且從構思到成書，都投入極大的心力。在編纂期間，特別延聘國內外教學權威，利用這套教材開班授課，由本公司全體編輯當學生，在學習出版門市部親自試用，以求發掘問題，加以修正。因此，這套教材的每一課都經過不斷的實驗改進，每一頁都經過不斷地字斟句酌，輸入中國人的智慧。

　　經由我們的示範教學證實這套教材，祇要徹底弄懂，受過嚴格要求者，英語會話能力定能突飛猛進，短時間內達到高效果。這套教材在編審的每個階段，都務求審慎，唯仍恐有疏失之處，敬祈各界先進不吝指正。

編者　謹識

CHARACTERS

Gloria Adams

Mark Jones

Marlene

John Smith

Teresa Lee

Bob Logan

Liz Davis

Tom White

Mike Young

Sofia Chang

Howard Young

Joyce Young

Loran Young

Sally Young

Ted Young

Lesson 1 Making Plans

Enjoy a day off.
Make a date with your friend.

(A) LET'S TALK

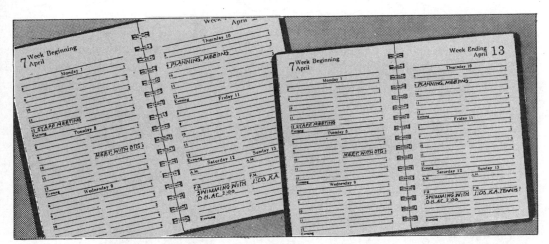

A : Teresa, do you have any plans for Saturday?

B : Nothing special. Do you have anything in mind?

A : Would you like to go bowling in the afternoon, and have something to eat afterwards?

B : That sounds like fun. But I think I'd rather make it in the evening.

A : OK. About what time should we meet?

B : Is 7:00 all right?

A : That'll be fine. At the fountain in the park?

B : Yes... Good.

A : So, see you then, Teresa. I've got to run.

B : Yes... Thanks, Bob. Bye.

LESSON 1

Conversation practice.
Use what you know.

🎧 (B) LET'S USE

- Additional Practice :

A : Hi, Bob. Are you busy tonight?
B : No, let's get together.

A : Would you like to go to the party tomorrow?
B : I can't. I have to study for a test.

LESSON 1

🎧 (C) LET'S PRACTICE

Here are some typical phrases you should know.

(1) **Setting Times and Dates** (informal)

1. What day would be good ? (*good = convenient*)
2. What about Wednesday ?
3. How about 11 : 00 ? (*i.e. What do you think of 11:00* ?)
4. I'm busy on Monday. How about Tuesday ?
5. Would the 14th be good ?
6. Let me check my schedule. Is Friday at noon good for you ?
7. Friday at 10 : 00 A.M.

8. Do you have any plans for Saturday ?
9. What are you doing Saturday ?
10. Do you have anything planned for Sunday night ?
11. What are you doing next Sunday night ?
12. What plans do you have for the weekend ?
13. Would you like to go to dinner tomorrow ?
14. Why don't we get together next week sometime ?
    (*i.e. Let's get together.*)
15. Let's try to see each other next month.

16. Do you have any free time in the coming weeks ?
    (*free time = available time*)
17. How would Wednesday morning be for you ?
    (*i.e. Is Wednesday morning convenient* ?)

18. Let's plan on lunch sometime next week.
    (*plan on = intend to*)

19. Do you want to get together and do something after work?

20. Would you like to go out sometime?
    (*go out = spend time together socially*)

(2) Setting Dates and Times (formal)

21. I'd like to invite you to dinner next Saturday.

22. Will Saturday afternoon at 3:00 be convenient?

23. I'd like to have you dine with me.

24. Will you call on me sometime next week?
    (*call on = make a short visit*)

25. Is 6 o'clock convenient for you?

26. I would be honored to have you join my table.
    (*join my table = have dinner with me*)

27. I would consider it a privilege to have you over for dinner.

28. Can I make an appointment with you sometime next week?

29. Let's do lunch sometime in the next few weeks.
    (*do lunch = have lunch*)

30. Shall we get together for lunch?

31. How would Tuesday be?

32. Could I drop by sometime this week? (*drop by = visit*)

33. Would you like me to drop by the office or shall we meet somewhere?

34. Where would you like to get together?

35. I would like to extend an invitation to you and your wife for dinner next week.

36. Will you be free for drinks on Friday at 7:00?
    (**be free** = *available* ; **drinks** = *alcoholic drinks*)

37. I wish to set up an appointment with you on Thursday.

38. What day would be convenient for you?

39. Let's meet at, say, around eightish.
    (**eightish** = *around eight o'clock*)

40. I would like to talk to you at your convenience.

41. How about meeting at the Hilton Hotel?

(3) Agreeing on Times and Dates (informal)

42. Friday would be good for me, too.

43. I can meet you on Wednesday.

44. I can't meet you then.

45. We will have to meet some other time.

46. Let's make it Friday at 10:00.
    (**make it** = *set the time and date at*)

47. I'm free all day Saturday.

48. I would love to join you for dinner.

49. Wednesday morning would be great for me.

50. I'm afraid I'm gonna have to decline. (**gonna** = *going to*)

51. I just can't make it this weekend.

52. I would love to be there, but I'm just too busy.

53. I accept your invitation.

(4) Agreeing on Times and Dates (formal)

54. We will accept your invitation.

55. This Friday is convenient for both of us.

56. We are delighted to accept your invitation.

57. 6:30 would be a much more convenient time for us.

58. We are honored to join you.

59. I feel honored to be a part of this.

60. I'm looking forward to joining you.
    (*look forward = anticipate with joy*)

61. Thursday is the worst day of the week for me.
    (*i.e. I'm very busy on Thursday.*)

62. Would you mind putting it off until Friday?
    (*put off = delay*)

63. Why don't we move it to Wednesday afternoon?
    (*move it = change it*)

64. That is a very inconvenient time for me.

65. I'm sure we can make it around eightish.

66. I'm afraid I'm booked solid this week.
    (*booked solid = no free time*)

67. We regretfully decline your invitation.

LESSON 1

(D) LET'S PLAY

Practice this role play.

1. You are talking to a friend. You are planning to go out for dinner together. You start. Begin like this:
" How about going out for dinner some time this week? "

2. Find a day when you are both free. (You are not free on Monday and Tuesday night.)

3. Decide what kind of food you'd like to eat. Decide on a restaurant.

4. Arrange a time and place to meet.

● **Here is an example dialogue. First, You are A; Your friend is B. Take turns practicing this dialogue.**

A : How about going out for dinner sometime this week?
B : _____

A : How about Wednesday, then?
B : _____

A : But I'm easy. How about you?
B : I went to a Chinese restaurant a couple of nights ago.
_____

A : I'd like to try that. Where is it?
B : _____
You know the place?

A : Great! And what time do you want to eat?
B : _____

LESSON 1

Exercise

Study the chart and answer the questions that follow. Try to make up your own questions to ask your partner.

Name	Sunday	Monday	Tuesday	Wednesday	Thursday	Friday	Saturday
Bob	go to a concert	go to the library	study math	clean the kitchen	wash the car	call Mike	paint the kitchen
Liz	wash the dog	call Sam	clean the yard	study English	fix the car	go to the movies	clean the bedroom
Mike and Ted	study math	go to the park	wash the car	go to a concert	study history	fix the car	go to the lake

Questions

1. What is Bob going to do on Thursday?
2. What is Liz going to do on Tuesday?
3. What are Mike and Ted doing this Sunday?
4. What will Liz do next Saturday?
5. When do Mike and Ted go to the lake?
6. When is Bob going to paint the kitchen?

Lesson 2 The Seasons

Talk about the seasons.
Plan a picnic.

(A) LET'S TALK

A : What a lovely day it is !

B : Yes, indeed ! And spring is just around the corner.

A : Yes. We had a bad winter, but it's almost gone. And now the days are getting longer. The weather is certainly beautiful. The flowers will be out soon. I think spring is the most pleasant season of all.

B : You know, they say that everything comes to life again in spring.

A : I'd like to go on a picnic next Sunday. How about you?

B : All right. Let's drive out into the country and find a little creek. We'll park there and walk along the stream.

A : Fine ! That sounds marvelous. I can hardly wait for next Sunday.

LESSON 2

🎧 (B) LET'S USE

Learn the names of the four seasons, the twelve months, the dates of the month, and the days of the week.

(1)

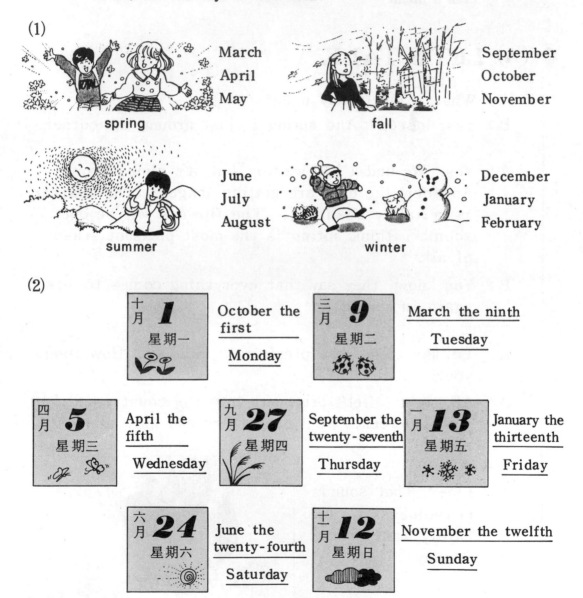

March April May — spring	September October November — fall
June July August — summer	December January February — winter

(2)

十月 **1** 星期一 October the first / Monday

三月 **9** 星期二 <u>March the ninth</u> / Tuesday

四月 **5** 星期三 April the fifth / Wednesday

九月 **27** 星期四 September the twenty-seventh / Thursday

一月 **13** 星期五 January the thirteenth / Friday

六月 **24** 星期六 June the twenty-fourth / Saturday

十月 **12** 星期日 <u>November the twelfth</u> / Sunday

* In colloquial English, people use " October one " instead of " October the first ".

* The Americans say " March the ninth (March 9)", whereas the Britons say " the ninth of March" or "ninth March (9 March)".

LESSON 2

(C) LET'S PRACTICE

Here are some useful expressions that you should know.

(1) Seasons

1. Which season do you like best?
2. What's your favorite season?
3. Are the seasons in your country similar to ours?

(2) Spring

4. What season is April in?
5. Today is the first day of spring.
6. What happens in the spring?
7. In the springtime, there is little rain, the grass turns green, and the flowers begin to bloom.
8. Spring is just around the corner.
   (*i.e. Spring will arrive soon.*)
9. Spring has come.

10. Spring has gone.
11. It's spring again.
12. Spring is here to stay.
13. The blossoms are now at their best.
14. Listen! Can you hear the birds singing in the trees?
15. We should go to the country and enjoy the natural surroundings.
16. The fresh air is good!
17. Happy Easter!

(3) Summer

18. Summer is here.

19. In the summertime, it's very hot and often very humid, but many people like to go on picnics, have beach parties, and go swimming. (**humid** = *the air is wet*)

20. Of all the seasons of the year, I like summer best.

21. Where are you going to spend your summer vacation ?

22. I can't stand the summer.

23. I just can't escape the heat.

24. The bugs are all over the place in the summertime. (**bugs** = *insects*)

25. My house is air-conditioned, so it's as cool as Alaska.

26. Yesterday it was exceptionally hot. Even in the shade, the temperature went up to 30 °C. (**shade** = *out of the sunshine*)

27. I'm glad the rainy season is over.

28. The rainy season lasted much longer than normal.

(4) Fall

29. In the fall, the leaves turn yellow, orange, and red, and then fall from the trees.

30. Fall is my favorite season.

31. I'm very fond of fall.

32. The temperature is just right, neither too hot nor too cold.

33. The autumn skies are fickle. (**fickle** = *unpredictable*)

34. The weather forecast says that the typhoon is turning in this direction.

(5) Winter

35. Merry Christmas !

36. Happy New Year !

37. Old man winter is here. (*i.e. winter has arrived*)

38. I hope it won't be too severe this winter.

39. Are you planning to go skiing during the holidays ?

40. I'm more fond of skating.

41. We enjoy having snow fights.
(**snow fight** = *a friendly battle using snowballs*)

42. Do you often catch a cold in winter ?

43. I take a cold shower every morning. It's a good way to keep fit.

44. Last Christmas, I spent the whole day at home with my family and relatives.

45. Christmas dinner is a special treat.

46. I'm looking forward to the arrival of Santa Claus.

47. What arc you going to give to your folks for a Christmas present ? (**folks** = *parents or relatives*)

48. Have the merriest of Christmases !

LESSON 2

(D) LET'S SING

Learn the song "The Months Of The Year" in English.

The Months Of The Year

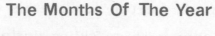

Snow in January

Ice in February Wind in March Showers in April

Buds in May Ros-es in June Play in July

Hot days in August School in Sep-tember Apples in Oc-tober

Cold days in No-vember Christ-mas — in De — cem — ber

LESSON 2

Exercise

Fill in the blanks. Write down either the date of the month or the day of the week.

1.

JULY						
S	M	T	W	T	F	S
						1
2	3	4	5	6	7	8
9	10	11	12	13	14	15
16	17	18	19	20	21	22
23/30	24/31	25	26	27	28	29

The meeting will be held on _____.
It's next _____.

2.

MARCH						
S	M	T	W	T	F	S
			1	2	3	4
5	6	7	8	9	10	11
12	13	14	15	16	17	18
19	20	21	22	23	24	25
26	27	28	29	30	31	

Their wedding anniversary is on _____.
It's this _____.

3.

DECEMBER						
S	M	T	W	T	F	S
					1	2
3	4	5	6	7	8	9
10	11	12	13	14	15	16
17	18	19	20	21	22	23
24/31	25	26	27	28	29	30

I left Taipei on _____.
It was last _____.

4.

JANUARY						
S	M	T	W	T	F	S
1	2	3	4	5	6	7
8	9	10	11	12	13	14
15	16	17	18	19	20	21
22	23	24	25	26	27	28
29	30	31				

I arrived in Boston on _____.
It was last _____.

5.

NOVEMBER						
S	M	T	W	T	F	S
			1	2	3	4
5	6	7	8	9	10	11
12	13	14	15	16	17	18
19	20	21	22	23	24	25
26	27	28	29	30		

He died on _____.
It was last _____.

6.

JUNE						
S	M	T	W	T	F	S
				1	2	3
4	5	6	7	8	9	10
11	12	13	14	15	16	17
18	19	20	21	22	23	24
25	26	27	28	29	30	

Jane's birthday is on _____.
It is next _____.

7.

OCTOBER						
S	M	T	W	T	F	S
1	2	3	4	5	6	7
8	9	10	11	12	13	14
15	16	17	18	19	20	21
22	23	24	25	26	27	28
29	30	31				

The graduation exercise will be held on _____.
It's next _____.

8.

FEBRUARY						
S	M	T	W	T	F	S
			1	2	3	4
5	6	7	8	9	10	11
12	13	14	15	16	17	18
19	20	21	22	23	24	25
26	27	28				

St. Valentine's Day is on _____.
It's next _____.

9.

SEPTEMBER						
S	M	T	W	T	F	S
					1	2
3	4	5	6	7	8	9
10	11	12	13	14	15	16
17	18	19	20	21	22	23
24	25	26	27	28	29	30

My birthday is on _____.
It was last _____.

Lesson 3
At the Hotel

Stay in a hotel.
Use English to get what you need.

(A) LET'S TALK

A : Good afternoon. I believe you have my reservation.

B : Your name, please ?

A : Howard Young, Y-O-U-N-G.

B : Oh, yes, Mr. Young. We have a single with bath for you. Now, will you fill in this card, please ?

A : Oh, surely. Incidentally, what time are the meals ?

B : Breakfast is from six to nine, lunch is from eleven to two, and dinner is from six-thirty to nine.

A : I see. And what's the check-out time ?

B : Twelve noon, sir.

A : OK. There you are.

B : Thank you. Now, I'll have the bellboy take you to your room.

A : Thank you.

LESSON 3

Here are some advertisements for three hotels.
Read them carefully.

(B) LET'S CHOOSE

HOTEL ROYAL ✿✿

☆ A SWIMMING POOL!
☆ THREE RESTAURANTS!
☆ A PRIVATE BEACH!
☆ TWO BARS!
☆ A DISCOTHEQUE!
☆ TWO ORCHESTRAS!
☆ A CASINO!
☆ FOUR TENNIS COURTS!

Park Hotel

tel. 7530790
3rd class
4 stories.
8 rooms with bath or shower
15 rooms without
no room service
radio in each room
dining room & bar
beach 25 minutes on foot
station 15 minutes by bus
single rooms from 300 NT.
twin rooms from 500 NT.

ALBERT HOTEL

tel. 8492018
1st class
4 stories
120 rooms, all with bath or shower
room service; T.V. in all rooms
restaurant, bar & dance floor
beach 15 minutes on foot
station 10 minutes by bus
single rooms from 800 NT.
twin rooms from 1200 NT.

● Now tell your partner which of these hotels you would prefer to stay in
and why do you chose it.

Examples : I would prefer to stay in_____because_____.

LESSON 3

🎧 (C) LET'S PRACTICE

Here are some typical phrases that you should know.

(1) Checking in

1. I think I'll probably be here for a week.
2. I don't have a reservation.
3. I'd like to stay a day longer.
4. I'd like a single room with bath for about 1000 NT a night.
5. Do you have any accommodation available at that price?
   (*accommodation* = *lodging, food, and services*)
6. Don't you have anything less expensive?
7. Could you give me a cleaner room, please?
8. Do you have any vacancies for tonight?
   (*vacancy* = *unoccupied room*)

9. Well, I'd like to help you, but I'm afraid all our rooms are taken.
10. This room will do. I'll take it.
11. The hotel charges 800 NT for an overnight stay.
12. Would you please register here?
13. Please fill out a registration card.
14. I want a sunny room. (*i.e. a room that gets lots of sunlight*)
15. A double-room suits me better.
    (*double-room* = *a room for two guests*)
16. What's the charge per night?
17. What kind of room do you want?
    (*respond with " A double-room," or " A single-room."*)
18. Please write your name, age, occupation, and home address on this slip.

(2) Room Service

19. I'd like some ice cream and two bottles of soda water, please.

20. Could I get a bottle of whiskey sent up and some glasses and ice?

21. I wonder if I could have a chicken sandwich and a glass of milk sent up, please.

22. I'd like breakfast in my room, please.

23. I'd like to have you call me at six tomorrow morning.

24. I wish to be called early tomorrow morning.

25. Wake me at six o'clock sharp.

26. There's no soap here.

27. We need another towel.

28. Please make up the room.

29. Would you please bring up some water?

30. Will you send these clothes to the laundry?

31. Can I still get something to eat at this time of night?

32. If you want breakfast in your room tomorrow morning, call Room Service tonight and place your order.

33. Could you take these dishes away?

34. I'd like to have breakfast in my room tomorrow.

35. Please cancel my order for tomorrow's breakfast.

36. Will you bring a pot of boiling water and three cups to Room 332?

(3) Checking out

37. I'm checking out now. Will you send someone for my baggage, please?

38. I'd like to pay my bill now, please. I will check out early tomorrow morning.

39. Would you get my bill ready?

40. Do you accept American Express cards?
(*American Express* = *name of credit card*)

41. Will you take a check?

42. Can I use VISA? (*VISA* = *name of credit card*)

43. Do you honor Master Card?
(*Master Card* = *name of credit card*)

44. Does the amount include the service charge?

45. May I have your key, sir?

46. Your bill comes to a total of $145.00.

47. There you are, sir. And here's your receipt. Hope you've had a nice stay here.

48. Can I pay three hundred dollars in traveler's checks and the rest in cash?

49. I'm leaving early tomorrow morning, so I'd like to settle my bill now. (*settle a bill* = *pay a bill*)

50. Here is the receipt and the change, sir.

51. Keep the change.

(4) Other Expressions You Should Know

52. This hotel is noted for its excellent accommodation, cuisine and service. (*cuisine* = *food*)

53. You're prohibited from smoking in bed.
(*prohibited* = *not allowed*)

54. This room has a very good view.

55. The porter will take your baggage up immediately.

56. Carry these two suitcases to my room.

57. Would you like to check your valuables ?
(**valuables** = *things of value*)

58. Is the dining room on the first floor or in the basement?

59. My room is very noisy. Can I change it ?

60. I'm sorry, I don't like this room. Could you show me another one ?

61. Where is the emergency exit and staircase ?

62. What's the check-out time ?

63. Are there extra blankets ? Sometimes I feel cold at night.

64. Is there a shoeshine service in this hotel ?

65. Are there any messages for me ?

66. I'm expecting a visitor at 3 o'clock. Please page me in the restaurant when he arrives. (**page** = *call*)

67. I want to keep my valuables in a safety-deposit box.

68. I've lost the key to my safety-deposit box.

69. I have some clothes to be washed. Do you take care of that ?

70. I'm leaving now. Could you send a bellboy to pick up my baggage ? (**bellboy** = *bellhop*)

LESSON 3

🎧 (D) LET'S LOOK

See the example and make your own questions and answers.

Example:

① Where do you come from? _____ _____
   ⇒ I come from America. _____ _____
② Where do you live?   _____ _____
   ⇒ I live in New York.   _____ _____
③ Where do you stay?   _____ _____
   ⇒ I always stay at the   _____ _____
      International Hotel.   _____ _____

● **Now answer these questions about yourself.**

1. What's your name? ....   4. Where do you live? ....
2. How old are you? ....   5. What's your job? ....
3. Where do you come from? ....   6. Where do you work? ....

● **Ask someone else these questions and fill in the form below.**

```
Name : ..................    Town/City : ..................
 Age : ..................          Job : ..................
Country : ..................    Place of work : ..................
```

LESSON 3

Vocabulary

Here are words you should know in a hotel.

(1) People in a Hotel

1. manager
2. bellboy
3. cashier [kæ'ʃɪr]
4. doorman
5. porter
6. tourist ['tʊrɪst]

(2) Types of Rooms

1. vacancy ['vekənsɪ]
2. a single room
3. a double room
4. a twin-bed room
5. suite
6. banquet hall

(3) Room Features

1. balcony ['bælkənɪ]
2. bath
3. shower
4. bathroom
5. drawers
6. dresser
7. toothbrush
8. toothpaste
9. pillow
10. light switch
11. bath mat
12. bath towel
13. bathtub
14. blanket
15. closet ['klɑzɪt]
16. coat hanger

(4) Room Registration

1. front desk; reception desk; registration
2. information desk
3. room key
4. room rate
5. register ['rɛdʒɪstɚ]
6. registration card
7. check in
8. check out
9. confirm [kən'fɝm]
10. identification card
11. nationality [,næʃə'nælətɪ]
12. occupation [,ɑkjə'peʃən]

LESSON 3

Exercise

Read the following dialogue and answer the questions.

A : International Hotel. Can I help you?
B : I'd like to reserve a single room for two nights.

A : When for?
B : July 23rd and 24th.

A : With bath or shower?
B : With bath if possible.

A : May I have your name please?
B : George Ferreira.

A : Could you spell that please?
B : F-E-R-R-E-I-R-A.

A : Thank you. I've reserved you a single room with bath for July 23rd and 24th. The room charge will be forty dollars per night.

B : I see. Thank you very much.

A : Thank you. Goodbye.

Questions :

1. What is the name of the hotel?
2. What is the reservation for?
3. What is the date of the reservation?
4. What is the man's name?
5. How much will it cost?

Lesson 4

Emotional Expressions

Read the dialogue.
Say how you feel.

(A) LET'S TALK

A : Bob, you look excited. What's going on?

B : I bought a lottery ticket, and they drew my number!

A : That's great! I'm very happy for you. What did you win?

B : I don't know yet. They're about to announce it on TV. Oh! I'm so nervous!

A : So it will be a surprise?

B : Yes! Shhh! They're calling my number now. I won ... a pair of movie tickets?!!

A : Hey! That's terrific! Congratulations!

B : No, it's not! The guy before me won two million dollars, and all I got was two movie tickets! I'm mad.

A : Don't be upset. Look, let's go out for a night on the town. Then you won't be so depressed.

B : Sure, why not? Wanna go see a movie?

LESSON 4

Read the cartoons.
Practice expressing your emotions.

🎧 (B) LET'S USE

LESSON 4

🎧 (E) LET'S PRACTICE

Here are some expressions you should know.

(1) Delight

1. Gee, that's great.
2. I'm so glad.
3. I'm so pleased!
4. I'm ever so happy!
5. How happy I am!
6. How pleased I am!
7. How glad I am!
8. How lucky!
9. How marvellous!
10. How wonderful!
11. Nothing could make me happier.
12. Thank God!
13. Thank Heaven!
14. That's nice!
15. Bravo!
16. Excellent!
17. I'm proud of you!

(2) Anger

18. Hell!
19. Damn it!
20. Go to hell!
21. You idiot!
22. Shame on you!
23. What a shame!
24. What a creepy guy! (*creepy = scary or disgusting*)
25. What a nuisance!
    (*nuisance = someone or something that annoys you*)
26. It gives me the creeps.
27. I'm so angry with you.
28. I'm so mad at you.

29. Don't you feel bad about it?
30. This is the limit.
31. I have no patience with you.
32. I'm out of patience with you.
33. No excuses.
34. Get out of my sight.
35. Get the hell out of here.
    (*hell = the place where bad people go when they die*)
36. How dare you say such a thing!
37. Mind your own business!

(3) Grief & Sympathy

38. That's too bad.
39. What a pity!
40. You poor thing.
41. How awful!
42. Ah, poor fellow.
43. What a sad thing!
44. I'm deeply grieved at the sad news.
45. Alas.
46. I'm so sad.
47. I'm sorry.
48. My deepest condolences. (*expression of sympathy*)

(4) Other Common Expressions

49. I'm surprised. What a surprise!
50. You look frightened.
51. He is bored.
52. It makes me upset.
53. She looks quite worried.
54. It depresses them.
55. The little girl looks lonely.

LESSON 4

🎧 (D) LET'S LOOK

Look at these pictures. Say how you think the people feel.

She looks amused.

He looks frightened.

He looks worried.

He looks embarrassed.

He looks disappointed.

● **Why do they feel this way? Because...**

This book is not interesting.

She lost her money.

An elephant is standing outside his house.

Her friend died.

She finished her homework.

LESSON 4

Exercise 1

In the first blank, choose the word which best describes how
that person feels.
In the second blank, explain why they feel that way.

1. He feels ⎡ _____ angry ⎤
             ⎢ _____ worried ⎥ because _____
             ⎣ _____ depressed ⎦

2. She is ⎡ _____ nervous ⎤
          ⎢ _____ delighted ⎥ because _____
          ⎣ _____ relaxed ⎦

3. He is ⎡ _____ scared ⎤
         ⎢ _____ depressed ⎥ because _____
         ⎣ _____ relaxed ⎦

4. He is feeling tired and ⎡ ____ frustrated ⎤
                           ⎢ ____ bored ⎥ because ____
                           ⎣ ____ satisfied ⎦

5. She ⎡ _____ feels very satisfied ⎤
       ⎢ _____ has mixed feelings ⎥ because _____
       ⎣ _____ is a little scared ⎦

6. He feels ⎡ ____ frightened ⎤
            ⎢ ____ annoyed ⎥ because _____
            ⎣ ____ surprised ⎦

LESSON 4

Exercise 2

Read the sentences.
Then think of a suitable reply.

1. A : I made A's in all my classes except one !
   B : _____ I'm very proud of you.

2. A : Unfortunately, I made a D in math.
   B : _____ There is no excuse for that.

3. A : Adam had a heart attack, but he's okay now.
   B : _____ He's a lucky man.

4. A : My dog died last night.
   B : _____

5. A : Sue and I have decided to get married.
   B : _____

6. A : The newscaster said another world war could break out at any
      moment.
   B : _____

7. A : Wake up ! The house is on fire !
   B : _____

8. A : My best friend got laid off today.
   B : _____ So many good people are losing their jobs.

Lesson 5 McDonald's Hamburger

To stay or to go.
Order your favorite fast-foods.

🎧 (A) LET'S TALK

A : Welcome to McDonald's. Are you ready to order ?

B : Yes, I would like a Quarter Pounder with cheese.

A : OK, and something to drink ?

B : Yes, give me a coke.

A : Large, medium, or small ?

B : Medium's fine.

A : Anything else for you today ?

B : Uh, how about a large French fries and a sundae ?

A : We have hot fudge, hot caramel, and strawberry.

B : I would like hot fudge, please.

A : All right. Is that for here or to go ?

B : Better make it to go.

A : OK. Your order will be ready in just a moment. Let me ring you up now.

LESSON 5

Conversation practice.
Use what you know.

(B) LET'S USE

LESSON 5

🎧 (C) LET'S PRACTICE

Here are some expressions you should know.

(1) Taking an Order

1. Can I take your order?
2. Are you ready to order?
3. Can I help you?
4. What would you like today?
5. What can I get for you?

(2) Placing an Order

6. I would like a Wendy's hamburger.
7. Give me a Big Mac.
8. I'll take a milk shake.
9. I want a medium coke.
10. How about a large order of french fries?

(3) Ordering Hamburgers

11. I want a double cheeseburger.
    (*double cheeseburger* = 2 *beef patties with cheese.*)
12. I want a hamburger with no onions.
13. Give me a Big Mac with extra catchup. (*catchup* = *ketchup*)
14. I'll have a Quarter Pounder; hold the mayo.
    (*hold* = *don't add* ; *mayo* = *mayonaise*)
15. I'll take a Chickenburger with extra lettuce and tomatoes.

(4) Ordering Drinks

16. I would like a cola, please.
17. Can you give me a coke with no ice?

18. I just want a glass of water.
19. I would like a chocolate shake. (*shake* = *milkshake*)
20. A coffee with cream, please.
21. I want two cartons of milk.

(5) Ordering Extras

22. Some chili with cheese, please.
23. I would like some of your corn soup.
24. And I would like an order of French fries.
25. Can I get some tomato catchup for my fries?
26. Would you mind giving me another order of onion rings?
    (*onion rings* = *fried onions*)
27. I want a chocolate sundae to go.
28. Can I have an extra order of fries?

29. Would you mind putting in some extra catchup?
30. I would like cheese with my chili.
31. Can you throw on some extra cheese? (*throw on* = *add a little*)
32. I want my hamburger with bacon.
33. Can you put on some cheese and bacon?
34. I want my burger with " the works."
    (" *the works* " = *all the ingredients for a hamburger* ; *the lot*)

(6) Problems

35. This order isn't right.
36. The hamburger is under-cooked. (*under-cooked* = *rare*)
37. My fries are cold.
38. This coke is flat. (*flat* = *not carbonated*)
39. The milk has gone sour.
40. I dropped my coke on the floor.
41. You have made an error in my order.
42. I said I wanted three hamburgers.

LESSON 5

🎧 (D) LET'S TASTE

Here are the foods you like to eat.

McDonald's Menu

Big Mac	Quarter Pounder with Cheese	Filet-o-Fish 〔fɪ'le〕	McChicken Sandwich	Cheeseburger French Fries
Chicken McNuggets	Egg McMuffin Apple Pie	Shake／CVS Sundae／HSP	Big Breakfast	Hash Brown Ice Cream Cone
Iced（Hot）Tea Iced（Hot）Coffee	Orange Juice Hot Chocolate	Coca Cola Sprite	Fanta Cherry Coke	Sausage McMuffin

- **Try to practise ordering food at McDonald's. Take turns being customers and waiters.**

  A：May I help you？   B：＿＿＿＿＿＿＿＿＿＿＿＿

  A：Is that all？   B：＿＿＿＿＿＿＿＿＿＿＿＿

  A：Is that to go or to stay？   B：＿＿＿＿＿＿＿＿＿＿＿＿

* *C＝chocolate   V＝vanilla   S＝strawberry*
  H＝hot fudge   S＝strawberry   P＝pineapple

(E) LET'S DISCOVER

Read the passage, then answer the questions that follow.

McDonald's USA

Fast-food restaurants are very popular in the United States. They are popular because the service is fast and the prices are low. Of all the fast-food restaurants, McDonald's is probably the most famous and the most popular.

" golden arches "

McDonald's is popular for several reasons : customers can get the same food at any McDonald's in any state; the employees are helpful and polite ; the tables and floors are clean; and people do like McDonald's food and service. David Green, one of its frequent customers, says, " McDonald's is my favorite place to eat in the whole world. I wouldn't move to a town that didn't have one. "

hamburger

fries & Coke

McDonald's Taiwan

The first McDonald's came to Taiwan in 1984. In the years that followed, McDonald's restaurants sprang up all over the island. Their growth rate was remarkable.

Why the big response? David Sun, the Managing Director of McDonald's Taiwan, claims that McDonald's came to Taiwan at the right time.

Ronald McDonald

The people of Taiwan are becoming more affluent and aware of the quality of life. McDonald's offers quality, service, cleanliness, and value. All of these factors have combined to produce a remarkable success story.

Happy Meal

In addition, McDonald's Taiwan has a strong local identity. They have done a lot of community and charity work, including its repeated donations to centers for mentally handicapped children and to the Children's Cancer Foundation. And McDonald's emphasis on being a part of the community has paid off. Every month over three million customers are served. Nevertheless, it still has to face competition from other fast-food restaurants on Taiwan, which now number over 500. But, as David Sun puts it, "We've only just begun."

Chicken McNuggets

McDonald's logo

Questions

1. Is McDonald's the most famous fast-food restaurant?
2. Is the food at every McDonald's the same?
3. Are McDonald's employees helpful and polite?
4. When did McDonald's come to Taiwan?
5. Does David Sun think that McDonald's came to Taiwan at a bad time?
6. Does McDonald's face any competition on Taiwan?

LESSON 5

Exercise

Put a check mark (√) in front of the sentence with the incorrect counting word for the noun.

1. Milk

____1. I'd like a glass of milk.

____2. I'd like a piece of milk.

____3. I'd like a bottle of milk.

2. Toast

____1. I want to have a glass of toast.

____2. Would you bring me a slice of toast?

____3. I'm eating a piece of toast.

3. Wine

____1. Bring us a bottle of wine.

____2. Would you like a glass of wine?

____3. Please have a plate of wine.

4. Rice

____1. I want another bar of rice.

____2. I'm eating a bowl of rice.

____3. Please join me in a plate of rice.

5. Ham

____1. Care for another slice of ham?

____2. Have another piece of ham.

____3. There is another scoop of ham on your plate.

LESSON 5

6. Cheese

_____1. Would you like me to cut you another slice of cheese?

_____2. I would like to buy a big piece of cheese.

_____3. Would you like a glass of cheese?

7. Pie

_____1. I would like a piece of pie with ice cream on top.

_____2. I'll take two slices of pie.

_____3. I could sure go for another drink of pie.

8. Beer

_____1. I would like another piece of beer.

_____2. Bring us three bottles of beer.

_____3. Bartender, I'll take a glass of beer.

9. Ice cream

_____1. I want to invite you for a dish of ice cream.

_____2. How many scoops of ice cream do you want?

_____3. Can I have another pot of ice cream?

10. Chocolate

_____1. I just ate a bar of chocolate.

_____2. I demand another pail of chocolate.

_____3. Can I have a piece of your chocolate?

11. Sugar

_____1. How many pieces of sugar do you want in your coffee?

_____2. He takes his coffee with two lumps of sugar.

_____3. I want two spoonfuls of sugar in my coffee.

Lesson  The Beauty Parlor

Get the style you want.
Speak to your beautician.

(A) LET'S TALK

A : I'd like a shampoo and a set, please.

B : Yes, ma'am. Just a moment, please.

B : All right, ma'am. This way, please. What style do you prefer?

A : Just the way I've been having it done, please.

B : Would you like a tight set?

A : No, I prefer a loose set.

B : You have a few gray hairs. Would you like me to color it?

A : Yes please. I didn't think they were noticeable.

B : They're not very noticeable. The coloring will also help your dry brittle hair.

A : I've been using a conditioner, but it doesn't seem to help. I have dry hair.

B : Do you use a blow dryer?

A : Yes, I always dry my hair with a blow dryer.

B : You should let it dry naturally. It's the blow dryer that makes your hair brittle.

LESSON 6

Conversation practice.
Use what you know.

🔊 (B) LET'S USE

LESSON 6

(C) LET'S PRACTICE

Here are some typical phrases that you should know.

(1) Giving Instructions

1. I'd like to make an appointment for a shampoo and a set.
    (**set** = *arrange the hair to a particular style*)

2. I made an appointment for a shampoo and a set.

3. I'd like you to give me whatever style is best for my face.
    (*i.e. cut the hair to compliment the facial shape*)

4. Just a haircut, please.

5. Please make it a bit shorter in the back.

6. Please set it in the same style.

7. I'd like a tight permanent.
    (**tight** = *many small curls*; *frizzy*; *permanent also called perm*)

8. I'd like a casual hairdo for sightseeing.
    (**hairdo** = *hair style*)

9. Please set it for a formal occasion.

10. I'd like it high over my forehead, and close to my head over the ears.

11. I want curls there.

12. I'd like a haircut. I think I'll try that little boy style.
    (**little boy style** = *short with bangs*)

13. I'd like a new hair style.

14. I'd like a trim today.

15. Trim the ends after the permanent, please.

16. Just shape it in the back.

17. I'd like a permanent, please.
18. I'm planning to let it grow.
19. I don't want a tight curl. Medium, please.
20. I want it parted on the left and absolutely flat on the top.
21. Don't put any oil on my hair.
22. Please give my hair a good scrub.
(*good scrub = thorough cleaning*)
23. Leave it as it is.
24. Puff the hair by teasing.
(*teasing = pushing the short hairs to the head with a comb*)
25. I want my hair dyed.

26. I want my hair bleached. (*bleached = made pale in color*)
27. I'd like a shampoo, cut and set.
28. If you think it suits my shape of face, go ahead.
29. I want to wear my hair long. (*i.e. I want long hair*)
30. I want a permanent wave.

31. I'll leave it entirely up to you.
32. Shampoo and hair cut, please.
33. While I'm in the dryer, I want a manicure, please.
(*manicure = trim and polish the fingernails*)
34. I want my nails a little longer and pointed.
35. Natural color polish, please. (*natural color = flesh tone*)
36. No polish. Just buff them, please.
37. I wish my hair were not so curly.

(2) Hairdresser's Questions

38. Lemon rinse or cream rinse, ma'am?
39. Shall I trim your hair a little?

40. How short do you want your hair?

41. What style do you like, ma'am?

42. Do you have any particular style in mind?

43. How about a shaggy dog cut?
    (**shaggy dog** = *unkempt like a dog*; **cut** = *style*)

44. How strong do you want your permanent?
    (*i.e. what degree of permanent*?)

45. Manicure? (*i.e. Do you want a manicure*?)

46. Facial? (*a treatment to improve facial appearance*)

47. Do you want me to thin out the top?
    (**thin out** = *make less dense*)

48. Do you want me to move the part?

(3) Problems

49. Can I make an appointment?

50. Can I make an appointment by phone?

51. Is this the latest hairstyle? (**latest** = *most modern*)

52. How much is it altogether?

53. My hair is very dry (oily, brittle).

54. Is it my turn?

55. Can I see some samples of hairstyles?

56. Which do you think would suit me best?

LESSON 6

🎧 (D) LET'S LOOK

Here are some essential beauty parlor terms.

(1)

① Farrah's style	② bubble	③ ponytail	④ straight hair	⑤ bangs
⑥ pigtails	⑦ Audrey Hepburn's style	⑧ permanent wave	⑨ Afro hairstyle	⑩ pinned up hair

(2)

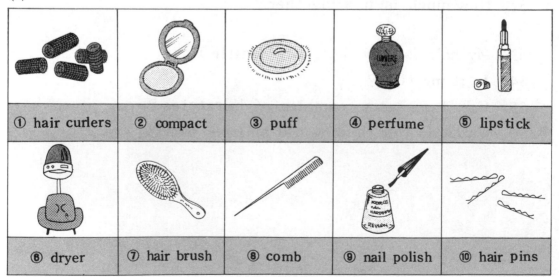

① hair curlers	② compact	③ puff	④ perfume	⑤ lipstick
⑥ dryer	⑦ hair brush	⑧ comb	⑨ nail polish	⑩ hair pins

LESSON 6

Vocabulary

Some additional beauty parlor vocabulary.

(1) <u>Hair Characteristics</u>

1. bangs
2. fringe
3. swinging bangs
4. braid
5. ponytail
6. pigtails
7. permanent wave
8. curly hair
9. fluffy hair
10. split ends
11. blond
12. brunette〔brunet〕

(2) <u>Cosmetics and Skin Conditions</u>

1. manicure
2. clear (natural) nailpolish
3. a pale nailpolish
4. nailpolish remover
5. nail
6. nail scissors
7. lipstick
8. a pale lipstick
9. eyebrow liner
10. eyebrow
11. tweezers
12. mascara
13. false eyelashes
14. perfume
15. astringent lotion
16. moisture lotion
17. skin lotion
18. cold cream
19. base foundation
20. normal skin
21. oily skin
22. dry skin
23. pimple
24. freckles
25. wrinkle
26. compact
27. cosmetics
28. face powder
29. facial
30. sunburn cream

(3) <u>Beautician's Terms</u>

1. rinse
2. hair spray
3. mousse
4. bobby pin
5. thinning
6. comb / brush
7. set
8. hair curler
9. shampoo

LESSON 6

Exercise

This is a role play exercise. Find a partner and take turns being the customer and the beautician. You may extend the dialogue if you like.

A : Hello, can I help you?
B : Yes,_____.

A : I have an opening now if you have time.
B : _____.

A : How do you want it cut?
B : _____.

A : There. What do you think?
B : _____.

• Here are some suggested phrases :

1. I'd like to make an appointment for a haircut.
2. Could you schedule me for a haircut?
3. Yes, I have time now.
4. Oh great! I can do it now.
5. Just a trim, please.
6. Short in the back and long on top.
7. Could you trim my bangs a little more?
8. Would you curl the back, please?

Lesson 7 Getting a Haircut

Speak with your barber.
Get the haircut you want.

(A) LET'S TALK

A : Next, please.

B : It's my turn, isn't it?

A : That's right. What'll it be?

B : I'd like a haircut and a shave.

A : All right. How would you like it cut?

B : Trim it short on the sides, but not too short in the back.

A : How about the top?

B : I think it could stand being a little shorter.

A : You don't want a crewcut, do you?

B : Oh, no, nothing that short.

A : Shampoo, sir?

B : Yes, please.

LESSON 7

Conversation practice.
Use what you know.

🎧 (B) LET'S USE

LESSON 7

(C) LET'S PRACTICE

Here are some typical phrases that you should know.

(1) Giving Instructions

1. Will I have to wait long?
2. Just a haircut, please. (*just = only*)
3. Just a haircut and shampoo, please.
4. Not too short, just a good trim.
5. Just a trim, please.
6. Rather short, please.

7. Cut it any way you think looks good, please.
   (*i.e. use your own judgement*)
8. I'd like it short around the neck and ears, please.
9. Please cut my hair in the same style it's in.
10. Fairly close on the sides, and a little off the top, please.
    (*i.e. short on the sides and long on the top*)
11. Don't take too much off the top.
    (*i.e. don't cut it too short on top*)

12. Short on the sides and on the top, please.
13. Leave the sideburns, and take quite a bit off the top, please.
14. Just part it a little more to the right.
    (*i.e. move the part to the right*)
15. No part, please. (*i.e. comb it straight back*)
16. I want the part on the left side.

17. Cut the sideburns fairly short, but leave the fringes as they are, please. (*fringe = edge*)

18. Could you shave a little more off the back, please?

19. Yes, clippers in the back only.
(*i.e. only use clippers when cutting the back.*)

20. Scissors on the sides.
(*i.e. only use scissors when cutting the sides*)

21. Not too short on top.

22. Not too short on the sides.

23. Not too much off, please.

24. Very short all over, please.

25. Just tidy it up a bit, please. (*tidy = neat and orderly*)

26. Without parting. (*i.e. no part*)

27. Cut more off the sides.

28. Can I get my hair cut?

29. My scalp feels itchy.

(2) Barber's Questions

30. Haircut, sir?

31. Shampoo, sir?

32. Hair tonic?

33. Shave?

34. Scalp massage?

35. How would you like it cut?

36. How shall I cut it?

37. Is that how you like it?

38. How about a shampoo?
(*i.e. Would you like me to wash your hair?*)

39. Do you want some spray?

40. Do you want me to use the clippers on the sideburns?
    (*clippers* = *electric razor*)

41. What kind of shampoo are you using?

(3) Paying the Fee

42. How much is a regular haircut without shampoo?

43. How much do I owe you?

44. Keep the change.

45. It's nice. Thank you.

(4) Trimming the Beard

46. Please trim my mustache.

47. Would you thin out my beard?

48. Can you trim my whiskers?

49. Leave the goatee, but shave everything else.
    (*goatee* = *short pointed beard on the chin*)

50. I would like to have muttonchops.
    (*muttonchops* = *side whiskers that are narrow at the temple and broad by the jaw.*)

(5) Hair Problems

51. I think you have eczema. (*eczema* = *common dandruff*)

52. I will give you something for your dandruff.

53. What can I do about my split-ends?
    (*split-ends* = *hair that is split at the end*)

54. Can you give me anything for brittle hair?
    (*brittle* = *break easily*)

LESSON 7

🗣 (D) LET'S LOOK

Here are terms you should know when you are in the barbershop.

(1)

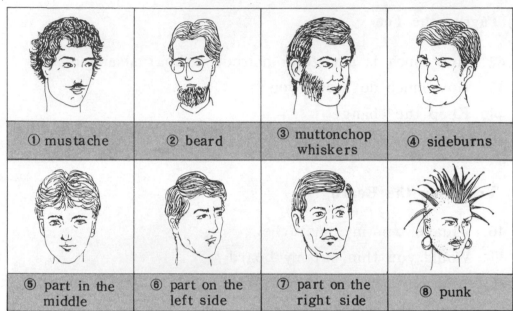

| ① mustache | ② beard | ③ muttonchop whiskers | ④ sideburns |
| ⑤ part in the middle | ⑥ part on the left side | ⑦ part on the right side | ⑧ punk |

(2)

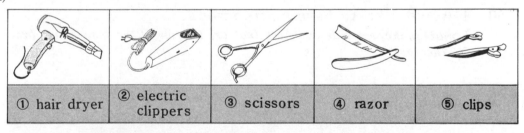

| ① hair dryer | ② electric clippers | ③ scissors | ④ razor | ⑤ clips |

(3)

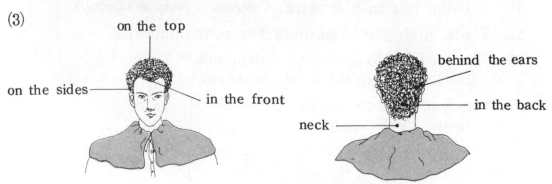

on the top

on the sides

in the front

behind the ears

in the back

neck

LESSON 7

Vocabulary

Here's a list of useful terms for the barbershop.

1. shave	13. dandruff ['dændrəf]	25. crew cut
2. shampoo	14. hair oil	26. scalp [skælp]
3. hair tonic ['tɑnɪk]	15. pack	27. spray
4. hair conditioner	16. shaving lotion	28. earpick
5. cologne	17. sides	29. comb
6. shaving cream	18. thin out	30. barber
7. after-shave lotion	19. towel	31. hair pieces
8. massage [mə'sɑʒ]	20. trim	32. head chair
9. bald	21. wig	33. scissors
10. bangs	22. electric clipper	34. barber chair
11. dye	23. haircut	35. hair brush
12. clip	24. color chart [tʃɑrt]	36. razor

LESSON 7

Exercise

This is a role play. Find a partner and take turns being the barber and the customer. As a customer, you should continue to instruct the barber on the way you want it cut. Here are some phrases you may use:

Barber

1. How would you like your hair cut?
2. Would you like a shampoo?
3. Do you want your bangs trimmed?
4. Would you like more off the top?
5. I can give you a shave if you like.

Customer

1. A little off the top, please.
2. Just a trim.
3. A shave and a haircut, please.
4. Could you trim the back a little more?
5. I want my hairstyle like the one in the picture.

● **Model dialogue. You may invent your own if you like.**

B : Good afternoon. _____ ?
C : Yes, _____ .

B : There, how do you like your haircut?
C : It's pretty good, but_____?

B : Sure. _____?
C : Yes, please.

B : There, how do you like that?
C : _____ .

Lesson 8 The Post Office

Mail letters and packages.
Speak with the postman in English.

(A) LET'S TALK

A : Good morning. May I help you?

B : I want to send these three letters by airmail to America, please. And I'd like three aerograms, too.

A : Sure. It's forty cents for each half-ounce letter, and thirty cents for each aerogram, totaling two dollars and ten cents.

B : Oh, I nearly forgot. How much is it to send this parcel to America?

A : Do you want to send it by airmail, or by surface mail, which takes more time to deliver but costs-less?

B : Airmail, please.

A : Then would you fill out this declaration form for customs? Write the contents of the parcel in this space, also the value of the items in this space.

B : Is this O.K.?

A : Yes, that's fine. That'll be ten dollars.

LESSON 8

🎧 (B) LET'S USE

Take the roles of a post-office clerk and a customer at a post office. You can use these expressions.

Customer

1. How much is an airmail letter to Korea, please?
2. How much does this parcel weigh?
3. I'd like to send this package by regular mail, please.
4. I'd like five airmail stamps, please.
5. When will this letter arrive in Korea?

Post-office Clerk

1. May I help you?
2. Let me check for you. Do you need anything else?
3. Here you are.
4. That comes to ten dollars.
5. It will arrive about the 22nd, sir.

● (C) LET'S PRACTICE

Here are some typical phrases that you should know.

(1) Mailing Letters

1. How much is it to airmail a letter to Japan?
2. Could you tell me how much it would cost to send this to France by regular mail?
3. How much more would it cost to send this special delivery?
4. I'd like to send this letter by registered mail, please.
5. What's the postage for this letter to Paris, please?
   (*postage* = *money paid to send a letter*)

6. I'd like to send this letter by sea mail, How much do you charge?
7. I'd like to send this letter to Japan by sea.
8. What's the charge on this express letter, please?
9. I want to register this letter.
10. When will this letter leave New York?
11. When will this letter arrive in France?

12. When is the post office open?
13. How much is first-class mail inside America?
14. How long will it take to get to Taiwan?
15. I want to have this letter registered. What is the registration fee?
16. Did I put enough postage on this?
17. Is there postage due on this?
18. Be sure to enclose the return postage.

(2) Sending Packages / Parcels

19. How much is a package to Brazil, please?
20. I'd like to send this box by parcel post, please.
21. I'd like to send this parcel by registered mail.
22. May I have this package registered, please?
23. Is sea mail just as safe?
24. Could you tell me how much to send this package to London?

25. Do I have to rewrap this package?
26. The contents of this package are breakable.
27. These are books. Can I get a special book rate?
28. How much does this parcel weigh?
29. I'd like to send this by parcel post.
30. Can this go by special delivery?

(3) Buying Postcards, Stamps, etc.

31. I'd like a 20¢ stamp, please.
32. I'd like five airmail stamps.
33. I'd like a book of 20¢ stamps, please.
34. I want ten post cards.
35. A 5 cent stamp, please.
36. An air letter, please. (*air letter = airmail letter*)

37. Half a dozen airmail labels and a book of stamps.
38. I'll have a registered envelope.
39. Which is the counter for stamps, please?
40. Can I have ten ten-cent stamps?
41. May I have a change-of-address card?

(4) Service

42. I'll have to check. Can I help you with anything else?

43. I'll look it up. Is there anything else?

44. Let me check for you. Do you need anything else?

45. Just a second. I'll have to check that. Anything else I can do for you?

46. Here you are.

47. Here you go.

48. I suggest you insure it if it's a valuable item.

49. I'll have a look. Did you want anything else?

50. That'll be 50 cents in all.

51. 50 cents exactly.

52. That comes to 50 cents.

53. Stamps are over at that counter.

54. Regular mail is 30 cents.

55. Express mail is 50 cents.

56. It's thirty cents on an ordinary letter.

57. Ten dollars for mailing and forty dollars for registry, so fifty dollars in all.

LESSON 8

🎧 **(D) LET'S PLAY**

You were standing in a post office when a robbery took place. The police are going to ask you some questions about what you saw. See how much you can remember.

1. Look at the picture for two minutes.

2. Close the book.

3. Answer the questions on next page.

NOW ANSWER THESE QUESTIONS. DON'T LOOK AT THE PICTURE AGAIN UNTIL YOU'VE FINISHED.

For example :

Where were you standing? (You)

(at the back, in the middle, at the front of the queue)

I was standing at the front of the queue.

Who was standing behind you?

(a woman, a man, a girl)

A woman was standing behind me.

Questions:

1. **What was the woman behind you wearing?   A**

(skirt and pullover, a jacket and a skirt, a dress)

2. **What was she holding?   A**

(a parcel, an envelope, a telegram)

3. **What was the customer at the counter sending?   B**

(a telegram, a letter, a parcel)

4. What was he wearing?   B

   (a suit, jeans and a shirt, jeans and a jacket)

5. What was the clerk giving him?   C

   (some stamps, an envelope, a form)

6. What were the two men coming into the post office
   carrying?   D and E

   (a suitcase, a parcel, a bag)

7. Who were they looking at?   D and E

   (you, the postman, the clerk)

8. What was the postman unlocking?   F

   (the front door, the safe, the postbox)

LESSON 8

Vocabulary

Here are some typical items that you should know.

(1) <u>Letters</u>

1. special delivery [dɪ'lɪvərɪ]
2. express delivery
3. general delivery
4. registered mail
5. registration fee [fi]
6. airmail
7. surface mail
8. sea mail
9. air letter
10. postage
11. return postage
12. Sincerely (yours)
13. Yours truly
14. Yours affectionately
15. Yours faithfully / Faithfully yours
16. Yours respectfully
17. P.S. = postscript
18. ZIP code
19. writing pad [pæd]
20. P.O. Box = Post Office Box
21. envelope ['ɛnvə,lop]
22. printed matter
23. aerogram ['eərə,græm]
24. charge
25. mailbox

(2) <u>Packages</u>

1. parcel ['pɑrsḷ]
2. mail order
3. package ['pækɪdʒ]
4. overweight
5. customs fee
6. fragile ['frædʒəl]
7. value
8. item
9. declaration [dɪ,klɛ'reʃən] form for customs

(3) <u>Stamps and Post Cards</u>

1. post card
2. postal card
3. a book of stamps
4. commemorative stamp
5. picture postcard
6. post-free
7. postmark
8. stamp-album ['ælbəm]
9. stamp-collector

LESSON 8

Exercise
Answer the questions below.

1. A: Where are your aerograms going to? (Australia, Germany, and Thailand)

   B: I'm_____.

2. B: How much is an aerogram to Japan? (Fifty cents)

   A: It_____.

3. A: Good morning. What do you have there? (3 letters to the U.S., 3 aerograms)

   B: I have_____, and I'd like _____.

4. A: What's in your parcel, and how do you want to send it? (clothes, cassette tapes, airmail)

   B: There are_____.

5. B: Is there any special way I need to wrap this parcel? (brown wrapping paper)

   A: Yes, you have to _____.

6. B: How long will it take for this package to reach New York by surface mail?
   (About 3 months at the longest)

   A: It _____.

7. B: How long will it take for this letter to reach India by air mail? (5 to 10 days)

   A: It_____.

8. B : How much does it cost to send a registered letter to
      Alaska? (Four dollars per half-ounce)
   A :_____ .

9. A : Do you want to insure this package?
   B : No,_____.
       / Yes,_____.

10. A : Would you please explain to me how to fill out this
       form?
       (the contents of your parcel, the value of the items)
    B : Of course, _____

       _____

Lesson 9 The Department Store

Go shopping.
Find what you are looking for.

🎧 (A) LET'S TALK

A : Can I help you today ?
B : Yes, I'm looking for a shirt.

A : What color would you like ?
B : Blue or yellow would be nice.

A : What size are you ?
B : I am a size 10.

A : OK. How about this one ?
B : I like the color, but I don't like the style.

A : I see. Well, what do you think of this one ?
B : It's very sharp. I'll take it.

LESSON 9

(B) LET'S LOOK

Answer the questions according to the picture below.

1. Where is the shoe department?
2. Can you tell me where the furniture department is?
3. Do you know where the casual wear department is?
4. Which way to the book department?
5. Where is the elevator?

Department Store

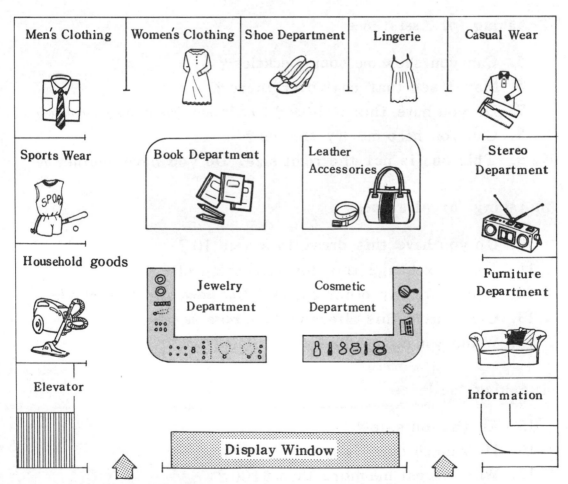

LESSON 9

🎧 (C) LET'S PRACTICE

Here are some useful expressions you should know.

(1) Asking Directions

1. What floor is the shoe department on?
2. Where is the cosmetics department?
3. Where is the nearest elevator?
4. Where is the dressing room?
   (*dressing room = place to try on clothing*)

(2) Asking for Assistance

5. Can you show me some neckties?
6. May I see that coat over there?
7. Do you have this in blue? (*i.e. same style in the color blue*)
8. Can you help me try this on?
9. This one is not the right size. Do you have another?

(3) Asking for Alternates

10. Do you have this dress in a size 10?
11. Can I exchange this for something else?
12. Are there any other colors? (*i.e. same style, different color*)
13. Can I have this altered? (*e.g. raise the hem*)
14. Would you make some alterations?

(4) Asking the Price

15. Is this on sale?
16. How much does it cost?
17. Will it cost me more than $100?
18. Do you have anything less expensive?

(5) **Problems**

19. I think there has been a mistake on this bill.
20. Would you check this bill again please?
21. I think you gave me too much change.
22. You forgot to add all of the items. (*add* = *total*)
23. This shirt has a hole in it.
24. A button is missing from this blouse.

(6) **Questions Asked by the Clerk**

25. Can I show you something else?
26. Would you like to see some other styles?
27. May I interest you in something? (*polite*)
28. Can I show you something?
   (*To all of the above, respond with* "No, thank you." " I'm just looking."
   or "Yes, please.")
29. Will there be anything else for you today?
30. Can I interest you in something else?
31. Will that be all?

32. About how much were you planning to spend?
33. What price range were you thinking of?
   (*respond with* " Between $10 and $20.")
34. Can you give me a ballpark figure? (*ballpark* = *rough estimate*)
35. How much are you willing to spend?
36. Did you have anything particular in mind?
37. Is this more like what you had in mind?
38. I have something here that might suit you better.
39. What were you thinking of?

LESSON 9

🎧 (D) LET'S DISCOVER

Read the passages, then answer the questions that follow.

Department Stores in the U.S.A.

What they have

America is probably the department store capital of the world. Across the nation every city, except for the small towns, has at least one department store. The largest department stores are known for the variety of goods and services that they offer. In these large stores not only can you buy clothes and household items, you can get your car repaired and have them put a fence around your house. Some of them even offer financial planning and insurance services.

What they are

Famous department stores are usually " chains. " In other words, the same store is located in many cities and towns. The most famous chain department stores in the U.S. include Sears, J.C. Penney, and the Bon Marche. These are the chains that offer the widest range of services. However, most department stores in the U.S. have only clothes and household goods like other department stores throughout the world.

Questions :

1. Name some of the things you can get at large department stores.
2. What is a chain?
3. What do most department stores in the US have?

Department Stores in TAIWAN

Local Department Stores

Taiwan is fast becoming one of the best shopping centers in Asia. The recent growth of Taiwan has left large numbers of people with time on their hands and money to spend. On the island there are many locally owned and operated department stores. The biggest of these, Tonlin and Far Eastern, are known for their ability to entertain. Within their walls are restaurants, movie houses, and playgrounds. This characteristic sets the department stores in Taiwan apart from the rest of the world.

Foreign Investment

This growth has also attracted foreign investments. Japan has been the leader here. The most recent department store to come to Taiwan from Japan is Sogo. It has a total of 15 stories and is fast becoming one of the best department stores in Taiwan. But while they may come from foreign countries, they all have the Taiwan flavor: basement food malls.

Questions :

1. Why is Taiwan becoming one of the best shopping centers in Asia?
2. Name one characteristic of Taiwan department stores.
3. What foreign country has a department store here?

LESSON 9

Vocabulary

Get more out of shopping by knowing these terms.

(1) Departments

1. men's clothing department
2. ladies' clothing department
3. sports wear
4. lingerie ['lænʒə,ri]
5. children's clothing department
6. junior miss department
7. men's shoes department
8. ladies' shoes department
9. children's shoes department
10. millinery ['mɪlə,nɛrɪ]
11. toy department
12. book department
13. electronics department
14. furniture department
15. household department

(2) Price

1. bargain sale
2. fire sale
3. inexpensive
4. cheap
5. sale price
6. fixed price
7. regular price
8. expensive

(3) Products

1. name brand
2. brand name
3. logo

(4) Sizes

1. extra small (XS)
2. small (S)
3. medium ['midɪəm] (M)
4. large (L)
5. extra large (XL)
6. too loose
7. too tight

(5) Fabric

1. flannel ['flænḷ]
2. cotton
3. blends
4. wool
5. silk

(6) Appearance

1. bright
2. dark
3. pattern
4. solid color
5. floral ['flɔrəl]
6. stripes
7. polka ['pokə] dots
8. plaid [plæd]

LESSON 9

Exercise

Take the roles of a salesperson and a customer in a clothing store.
You can use these expressions.

Customer

1. I would like to see some sweaters.
2. Can you show me your jackets?
3. Do you have this dress in a size 9?
4. Do you have one in a darker color?
5. I'll take this one.

Salesperson

1. May I help you?
2. What color would you like?
3. Here's a dress in your size.
4. You can try it on over there.
5. How does it fit you?
6. We don't have any left, but I can order some for you.

Lesson 10 An Evening at the Theater

Spend an evening out.
Talk about the play in English.

🎧 (A) LET'S TALK

A : Would you show me your tickets, please?

B : Right here.

A : Follow me, please. ......
Here's your seats, sir.
The performance will be starting in five minutes.

(*during the intermission*)

B : Excuse me. How long is the intermission?

A : It's for fifteen minutes, sir.

B : Where can I buy the program?

A : At the information counter over there.

B : Thank you.

(*after the performance*)

B : How did you like the performance?

C : I enjoyed it very much.

LESSON 10

Conversation practice.
Here are some basic phrases for the theater.

(B) LET'S USE

LESSON 10

🎧 (C) LET'S PRACTICE

Here are some phrases you need to know.

(1) At the Box Office

1. I want two tickets for this evening.
2. Do you have any seats for tomorrow afternoon?
3. I'd like to have six seats in the balcony.
4. I want seats on the main floor down front, and in the center of the row.
5. Are there any seats left for Saturday night?
6. Can I still get tickets for tonight's show?
7. I want two tickets in the 4th row.

8. I'd like two seats together. (*i.e. side by side*)
9. May I have box seats, please?
    (*box seat = a seat in a box; usually the best seats in the theater*)
10. How much are the tickets?
11. We have seats in the second balcony.
12. All seats are sold.
13. Advanced sales begin on Friday.

(2) Showtimes

14. When does the show start?
15. What time does the show begin this evening?
16. What time will the show let out? (*let out = be over*)
17. What time do the doors open?
18. The show begins at 7:30.

19. It already began ten minutes ago.

20. Will it be long before the curtain rises ?
    (*curtain rises = show begins*)

21. The curtain is up now. (*i.e. the show has begun*)

(3) About the Seats

22. Could you show us our seats, please ?

23. I can't find my seat. Could you help me ?

24. First aisle to your right, please.
    (*i.e. In the first aisle on the right hand side*)

25. They are in this row, the fifth and sixth seats.

26. You can take the elevator to get to the third floor.

(4) About the Intermission

27. There's an interval (intermission) of ten minutes.

28. How long is the intermission ?

29. The intermission is for fifteen minutes.

30. The performance is about to begin. Please take your seat.

31. They're blinking the lights. We'd better go back to our
    seats. (*blinking = turning the lights on and off*)

(5) Talking about the Performance

32. How do you like the performance ?

33. It's a drama well worth seeing. (*i.e. very good*)

34. I love the music and the costumes, and settings are
    wonderful, too.

35. I think he is one of the leading female impersonators.

36. The stage decorations are magnificent.

37. They are in gorgeous costumes. (*gorgeous = very beautiful*)

38. Most of the spectators seem to be moved to tears.
   (*moved to tears = started crying*)

39. I think the cast sounds a little bored with the songs.

40. What's your favorite song in the show so far?
   (*so far = up to now*)

41. I enjoyed it very much.

42. I'm enjoying every minute of it.

43. What's the name of the song they've just played?

44. Did you think that the lead actor was a little weak?
   (*weak = did not deliver a strong performance*)

45. I thought the plot was well-crafted, didn't you?

46. What was your impression of the lead actor?

47. Do you think that the play could have been improved?

48. That was a marvelous performance. We will have to see it again.

49. I didn't like their interpretation of Shakespere's "MacBeth".

50. I couldn't understand their lines, could you?
   (*lines = sentences that actors speak*)

51. Why did you like it so much? I hated the play.

52. The acting was bad; the singing was bad; and the sets were bad.

53. That was the worst play I've ever seen.

54. What a pile of trash! (*i.e. It was really bad*)

LESSON 10

🎧 (D) LET'S LOOK

Point to each number and say what it is outloud.

① stage	⑬ front row seat
② actor	⑭ audience
③ actress	⑮ usher
④ cast	⑯ auditorium〔,ɔdə'tɔrɪəm〕
⑤ curtain	
⑥ wing	**Other words you should know**
⑦ spot light	① outer lobby
⑧ orchestra seat〔'ɔrkɪstrə〕	② intermission〔,ɪntə'mɪʃən〕
⑨ setting	③ program
⑩ dress circle	④ opera
⑪ stall	⑤ aisle
⑫ balcony seat	⑥ row

LESSON 10

🎧 (E) LET'S READ

Read the passage and answer the questions that follow.

PEKING OPERA

While singing is the most obvious form of expression used in Peking opera, there are many other forms. Other expressions are pantomime and acrobatics. The stage doesn't have very many stage props. Chairs and tables can be mountains, bridges, thrones, or beds. These few stage props, along with costumes and make-up, are the opera's main vehicles of expression. The stories themselves are drawn from ancient legends and historical events, and are complete with good guys and bad guys. These roles are clearly defined by the clothes and make-up they wear. In addition there are over fifty hand-movements made by the actors which are all symbolic. In all, each of these forms of expression make Peking opera unique among the world's theatrical forms.

* *pantomime = to tell a story with body and face movements*
* *acrobat = one who performs difficult physical actions*
* *prop = furniture or objects used on a theater stage*

1. What is the most obvious form of expression used in Peking Opera?
2. What are some other forms of expressions used?
3. Where do the stories for the opera come from?
4. What do the actors use to define their roles?
5. What makes Peking opera unique in the world?

LESSON 10

Exercise

Finish the dialogue using the words in parentheses.

1. Do you have any tickets for this evening?
   (booked up) _____ .

2. What time is showtime?
   (7:30) _____ .

3. I can't seem to find my seat.
   (help you) _____ _____ .

4. Where will you be sitting?
   (row 36) _____ .

5. How did you like the play?
   (very funny) _____ .

6. Who played the role of "Mary"?
   (Nancy Brown) _____ .

7. How long will the intermission be?
   (fifteen minutes) _____ .

8. Do you know who is the director of this play?
   (check my program) _____ .

9. What do you think of the set?
   (magnificent) _____ .

10. That was a moving performance, don't you think?
    (agree with you) _____ .

Lesson 11 The World of Sports

Join the team.
Speak about your favorite sports.

🎧 (A) LET'S TALK

A : Do you like tennis?

B : I'm afraid not. I've never played it.

A : What kinds of sports do you like?

B : Oh... soccer, riding.... I really enjoy riding.

A : Uh huh. I guess that can be fun... once in a while. I don't go for baseball, though.

B : Oh I do. It's great fun — though football is my favorite sport.

A : Have you ever played on a team?

B : No, I never played on a team. But I like to get together with my friends and play. How about you?

A : I used to be on the soccer team.

B : Oh really? Did you win any medals?

A : Yes, our team got second place in the state soccer meet.

B : That's wonderful.

LESSON 11

Conversation practice.
Use what you know.

(B) LET'S USE

(1) A : Do you play baseball ?   B : No, I don't.

   A : What do you play ?   B : I play _____

Softball   Badminton   Football   Ping-pong   Handball

Rugby   Golf   Tennis   Volleyball   Soccer

(2) I started to practice _____ last year.

Boxing   Judo   Speed skating   Skiing   Jogging

Karate   Fencing   Weight lifting   Gymnastics   Rowing

LESSON 11

🎧 (C) LET'S PRACTICE

Here are some typical phrases that you should know.

(1) Sport

1. What's your favorite sport?

2. What sport do you play?

3. What sports did you take part in at school?
(*take part in* = *participate in*)

4. What sports did you participate in at high school?

5. What sports did you go in for when you were young?
(*go in for* = *participate in*)

6. I'm no athlete.

7. The successful player is always on his toes.
(*on his toes* = *alert*)

8. Our team walked off with the championship.
(*walk off with* = *win without difficulty*)

9. We won the game, but it was a narrow squeak.
(*a narrow squeak* = *win by a narrow margin*)

10. They've got no team spirit.

11. Do you actually play or do you just watch?

12. The Olympic Games are held every four years.

13. Do you have any interest in the Olympics?

14. How do you keep fit? (*fit* = *healthy*)

15. Getting some exercise is good for the health.

16. I'm practicing sports that keep me going all year round.
(*keep me going* = *help me stay healthy*)

17. What sports do you play for your health?

(2) Football, Soccer

18. All he ever thinks about is football.
19. I played soccer in high school.
20. How was the game?
    —— Our team was badly beaten.
21. What was the score?
    —— Nine to zero.
22. Have you played soccer since then?
    —— Yes, but only from time to time.
23. What position do you play?
24. What position are you in? (*i.e. what position do you play?*)

(3) Badminton

25. Badminton is a game from England.
26. I have some badminton rackets.
27. Do you have a badminton birdie? (*birdie = shuttle cock*)
28. Let's hit the shuttle-cock back and forth.
29. That was a good volley. (*volley = hit the ball before it bounces*)
30. The birdie is supposed to go over the net, not through it.

(4) Ping-pong or Table Tennis

31. How about a game of ping-pong?
32. Let's play a game to 21. (*i.e. play until a player reaches 21 points*)
33. You have to win by two points.
34. Hold the ping-pong paddle this way.
35. The ball touched the net; serve again.
36. You hit the ping-pong ball too hard. It's broken.
37. You put a lot of spin on that ball.

(5) Tennis, Golf

38. I'm on the tennis team at college.

39. Is the subscription for the tennis club very high?
(*i.e. cost a lot*)

40. A tennis match was held on our school court yesterday.

41. Do you play golf?

42. What's your golf handicap?
(**handicap** = *points given or taken away to equalize the chances of winning*)
—— My golf handicap is 19 at the moment. But I hope to improve.

(6) Billiards

43. How about a game of pool?

44. I will put the 3 ball in the corner pocket.

45. Here's a combination shot.
(**combination shot** = *sinking a ball with a secondary ball, and not the cue ball*)

46. I'm going to bounce the cue ball off the cushion and hit the 5 ball.

47. Hand me that cue stick.

48. Rack the balls for another game. (**rack** = *gather and organize*)

49. Where's the chalk? I need to chalk the tip of my cue.

(7) Skiing and Skating

50. Do you like skiing?

51. I always go skiing in winter.

52. Do you ever go skating?
—— I've never tried it, but I'd like to.

53. Can you go skating with me this weekend?

(8)　Jogging

54.　Let's go for a jog.

55.　I need a pair of comfortable jogging shoes.

56.　Where is a good place to run?

57.　I jog five kilometers a day.

58.　You should warm-up before jogging.
　　　(*warm-up* = *do exercises and stretch muscles before jogging*)

59.　You should jog at a comfortable pace.

60.　Jogging is great exercise.

(9)　Boxing

61.　Did you watch the boxing match on television last night?
　　　—— Of course, I didn't miss it.

62.　I went to watch a boxing match.

63.　I watched a boxing match on TV last night.

64.　The World Lightweight Champion was knocked out in the
　　　9th round.

65.　He was floored with a right uppercut to the jaw.
　　　(*floored* = *knocked out*; *uppercut* = *a hit directed upward*)

66.　Why not throw in the towel? (*i.e. quit*)

67.　If he is in form, he will win the match.
　　　(*in form* = *in good physical condition*)

68.　Boxing is a sport which develops our muscles.

LESSON 11

🎧 (D) LET'S READ

Read the passage, then answer the questions that follow.

THE OLYMPIC GAMES

Every four years the world turns its attention to the Summer and Winter Olympic Games. It is a time when the countries of the world stop showing their military strength, and start showing their physical strength. The modern Olympic Games began in 1896 when athletes from thirteen countries came to Athens, Greece to compete. But the first Olympic Games were held about 2,700 years ago in Greece. Like today, the games were held every four years and were important events. But after hundreds of years the athletes wanted to play for money, and the games were stopped. For 1,500 years there were no Olympic Games.

1. When did the modern Olympic Games begin?
2. How many countries came to the first modern Olympic Games?
3. When were the first Olympic Games held?
4. Where were the first Olympic Games held?
5. Why were the games stopped for 1,500 years?

LESSON 11

Exercise

Read these rules for popular sports. Match the pictures to the sports.

☐ The object is to move a ball into the other team's goal by hitting it. The player can use any part of his body except his hands or arms.

a. Badminton

☐ Each team has from one to four players. The object is to volley the birdie back and forth over a net without letting it touch the ground. The players use long-handled rackets.

b. Volleyball

☐ Either two or four players can play. The ball is allowed to bounce only once on each side. The server gets two chances to serve the ball over the net into the service area.

c. Tennis

☐ No player may touch the net. The ball cannot be hit more than three times by a team, nor can the same person hit it two times in a row.

d. Golf

☐ This is played on a course with clubs and balls. Players try to hit the ball from the tee to the hole. The object is to do this with the least number of hits, or strokes.

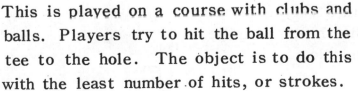

e. Soccer

Lesson 12 Public Transportation

Visit the ticket counter of a passenger ship.
Buy a ticket to the U.S.

🎤 (A) LET'S TALK

A : Is this where I book for the States ?

B : Yes, sir. This is the passenger department. Where do you want to go ?

A : I wish to go to San Francisco and would like to leave Korea in June.

B : Yes, sir. Then what about the *Cleveland* ?

A : Are there any spare cabins about the second week in June ?

B : Do you want first or second class, sir ?

A : First, please. I'm taking my wife with me.

B : Then you'll need a two berth cabin, sir ?

A : Yes, and I'd like it as near amidships as possible, for my wife's a bad sailor.

B : Here is good cabin, sir. It's in a very quiet place on the ship, and quite in the middle.

A : Yes, it looks nice.

LESSON 12

🔊 (B)LET'S LOOK

**Here are some useful transportation terms.
Which way would you like to travel ?**

(1) **Train**

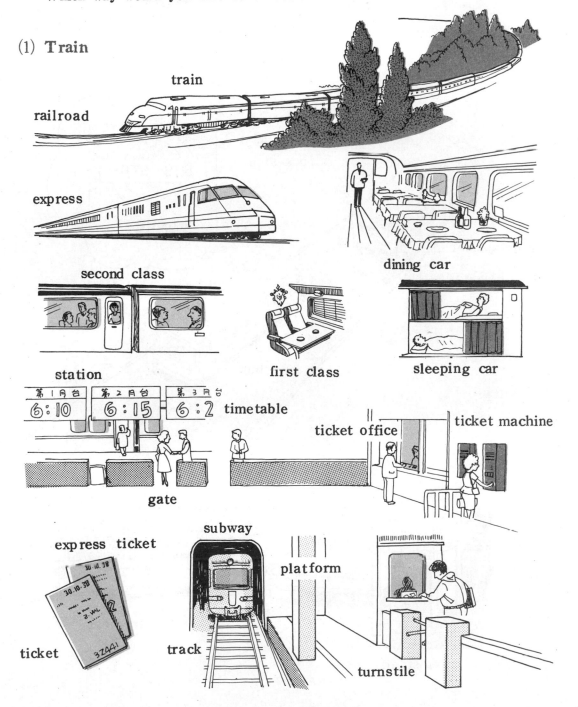

train

railroad

express

dining car

second class

station

first class

sleeping car

timetable

ticket office

ticket machine

gate

express ticket

subway

platform

ticket

track

turnstile

(2) **Bus**

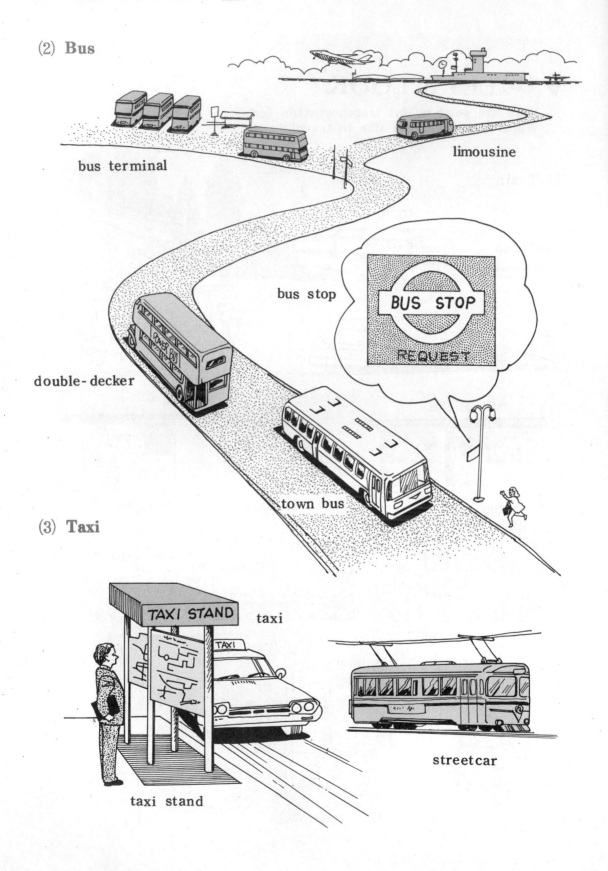

bus terminal

limousine

bus stop

BUS STOP

REQUEST

double-decker

town bus

(3) **Taxi**

TAXI STAND

taxi

TAXI

taxi stand

streetcar

(4) Ship

cargo boat

sailing ship

freighter

container ship

passenger ship

wharf / pier

port

dock

LESSON 12

🎧 (C) LET'S PRACTICE
Here are some typical phrases that you should know.

(1) Train, Subway

1. Two tickets to Denver.

2. I'll take two tickets for the first class on the special super express.

3. There is an express for Chicago at 11:00 tonight.
   (*express = faster than others, or with fewer stops*)

4. When does the 8:20 express arrive in Washington?

5. I want to reserve a berth on the eleven o'clock night train for New York tomorrow.
   (*berth = a space to sleep on a train*)

6. Can I reserve two second-class seats, please?

7. Can I reserve a seat on the train for Evanston?

8. Are there vacant berths on the train leaving for Washington at ten this evening? (*vacant = empty*)

9. How far are you going?

10. Here comes the train.

11. The trains run every three minutes during the rush hour. (*rush hour = busiest traffic time*)

12. I'd like to stop off at Denver.
    (*stop off = interrupt your trip without paying extra*)

13. Can I stop over wherever I like?

14. Do we have to transfer at Oklahoma City?
    (*transfer = change trains*)

15. Do we have to change trains at Springfield?

16. Give me a half-ticket for my child.
    (*half-ticket = child's ticket*)

17. I want a first class ticket to Chicago, please.
18. One way or return ? (*return ticket = round-trip*)
19. What's the express charge ?
20. How much is a round trip from Chicago to Detroit ?
—— By train it's about 50 dollars.
21. To get on a first class, you must pay more.
22. I don't have an express ticket.
23. Buy an express ticket on the train.
24. What time is there a train to Chicago early tomorrow ?
—— There's an express at seven.
25. When is the express for Chicago due here ?

26. When is the next special express to San Francisco ?
27. There is a special super-express at nine.
28. Any train will be all right.
29. All seats are sold.
30. They've just announced over the loudspeaker that the train is twenty minutes late.
31. How many hours earlier can we get to New York by express than by ordinary train ?
32. Is there a dining car on the 10:00 train to Boston ?

33. Is this seat taken ?
34. Can I get on this train with this ticket ?
35. Your ticket is out of date. (*out of date = not good any more*)
36. Don't lean out of the window.
37. I'm afraid I've taken a wrong train.
38. Is this an express train or a local train ?
39. Does this train go to Birchwood ?
40. Will the next one be very crowded ?

41. How many more stops to Western Springs?
42. Your train leaves on Track 3.
43. Which is the platform for the 10:10 express to Portland? (*platform* = *a raised area people stand on*)
44. The platform for the 11:30 express to Denver is No. 27.
45. I'm taking the 11:30 express to Denver.
46. May I see your ticket, please?
47. Excuse me, but let me see your ticket.
48. Where are we now?
    —— We have just passed Omaha.
49. We arrive in five minutes.
50. The doors open on the right side.

(2) Bus

51. Does this bus go to the station?
52. Is this the right bus for the Town Hall?
53. Do you go to St. Mary's Church?
    —— No, you'll have to get off at the post office, and take a 25.
    —— No, we only go as far as the park, but you can walk from there.
    —— No, you're going the wrong way.
    —— No, you should have caught a 20.
54. Jump out at the bridge and get one there.
55. How much further is it?
56. Have we got much further to go?
57. Please tell me where I should get off.
58. Could you tell me when we get there?
    —— It's the next stop.
59. Can you tell me where to get off?
60. It's quite a way yet, but I'll tell you in good time.

61. It's four stops after this one.

62. Let's go downtown by bus.

63. Let's take the bus downtown.

64. What's the next stop?

65. The bus is to arrive here at one.

66. Does this bus go along Michigan Avenue?

67. How much is the fare?

68. You'll have to transfer to No. 12 at Oak Street.

69. Will you tell me what the name of the second stop is?

70. How often does the bus for downtown run?
—— About every four or five minutes.

71. We'd better take the next bus.

72. This one's full.

73. Will there be another bus soon?

74. Is that my bus?

75. You have to get off at the next stop and take another bus.

76. I have ridden past my stop.

77. Will this bus take me downtown?

78. Can I get off in front of the National Museum?
—— I'm sorry, but we don't make a stop there.
—— You will have to ride as far as Chicago station.

79. Please hold on to your straps. We're coming to a sharp turn.
(*straps* = *leather loops hanging from the ceiling of a bus, for people to hold on to*)

80. Please don't stand on the step.

81. Please don't get off until the bus has stopped.

82. Please move up a little further.

83. Would you please move to the back of the bus?

(3) Taxi

84. Call me a taxi, please.
85. Can I get back to my hotel quickly from here by taxi?
86. Can I catch a taxi any place I like?
87. Please take me to the International Airport.
88. Keep the change, please.
89. I will pay as much as it says on the meter.
   (*meter* = *a machine that displays your fare*)
90. Let me off here, please.

(4) Ship

91. Are there any spare cabins on the ship for Vancouver?
   (*cabin* = *a room on a ship*)
92. I'd like to book a passage for London via Hong Kong.
   (*via* = *through, by way of*)
93. Are there any supplements to pay on board?
94. Do you have any discounts for couples?
95. We're leaving Marseilles for New York on the Queen Elizabeth tomorrow.
96. Welcome aboard.

LESSON 12

🎧 (D) LET'S LEARN

(1) **Read the timetable, then practice your own conversation.**

Train timetable Mondays — Fridays			
Platform	Destination	Departure	Arrival
5	Birmingham	8.30	10.00
7	Manchester	9.00	11.30
3	Chester	9.30	12.00
8	Rugby	10.00	11.00
9	Glasgow	11.00	4.00 (16.00)
6	Liverpool	11.30	2.00 (14.00)

● **Ask and answer questions about the trains like this:**

1. What time does the Manchester train leave?

....

2. It leaves at nine o'clock.

....

3. Which platform does it leave from?

....

4. Platform number seven.

....

5. And how long does the journey take?

....

6. It takes about two and a half hours.

....

(2) **Read the following patterns, then practice your own sentences.**

Present perfect tense.

Affirmative Statements

I You We They	have ('ve)	been here for an hour.
He She	has ('s)	already arrived.

Negative Statements

I You We They	haven't	been here long. arrived yet.
He She	hasn't	

1. I _____ (not buy) a train ticket for New York yet.

2. They _____ (announce) over the loudspeaker that the train is twenty minutes late.

3. I'm afraid you _____ (take) the wrong bus.

4. _____ (you have) lunch already?

5. She _____ (live) here for ten years.

LESSON 12

Exercise

Please look at the picture, then answer the questions which follow.

88 ——————— 608 — — — — —
203 — — — — — 232 ··················
937 ——————— bus stop ●

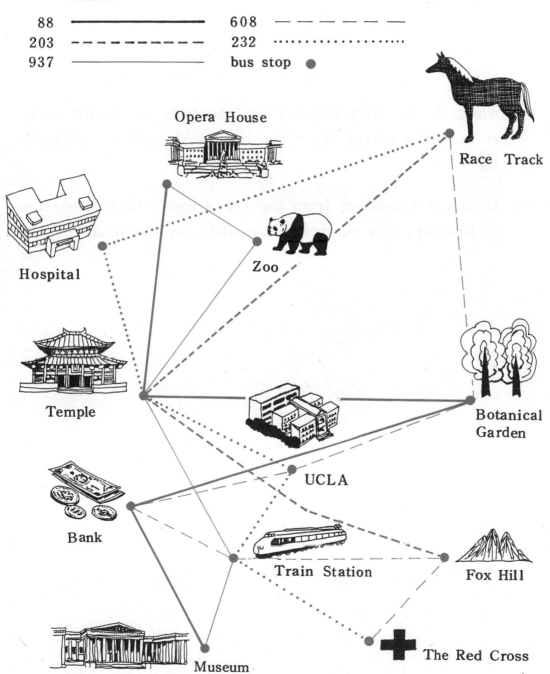

Opera House

Race Track

Hospital

Zoo

Temple

Botanical Garden

UCLA

Bank

Train Station

Fox Hill

Museum

The Red Cross

Questions

1. You are a student at UCLA, and work at the racetrack after your classes are over. What bus would take you there with the fewest stops ?

2. You want to travel from the bank to the temple. Which route would cover the shortest distance ?

3. What is the least number of transfers you would have to make to travel from the botanical gardens to the zoo ?

4. If you're travelling from the opera house to the museum on bus 88, how many stops would your bus make ?

A Visit to the Doctor

Visit the doctor.
Tell him how you feel.

(A) LET'S TALK

A : How do you feel today?
B : I feel awful. I have a sore throat and a headache.

A : Let me take your temperature. Put this under your tongue.
B : What does it say, doctor?

A : It reads 38.8°C. You have a fever. Do you have a cough, too?
B : No.

A : A stomachache?
B : No, but it is a little upset.

A : I think you probably have the flu. I've seen many cases of it recently. Let me examine your throat and listen to your chest. Stick out your tongue and say "aaaaah".
B : Aaaaaaaah.

A : It looks a little red. I'll give a prescription for some medication that will make you feel better. But the best medicine is to stay home in bed and drink plenty of fluids.
B : OK. Thank you, doctor. Bye.

A : Not at all. Remember to take it easy. It should only last a couple of days.

LESSON 13

🎧 (B) LET'S LOOK

Conversation practice.
Use the new vocabulary in this dialogue.

A : What's the matter?
B : I have _____ . / I've got _____ .

a stomachache	a headache	an earache	a sore throat
a cold	a cough	the flu	a fever

Now use the vocabulary in these dialogues.

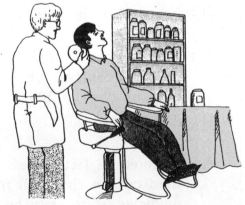

Doctor : Mike, you look terrible.
Mike : I have the **flu.**

Doctor : I can't find anything wrong with you.
Howard : But why do I have a terrible **earache**?

LESSON 13

(C) LET'S PRACTICE

Here are some typical phrases that you should know.

(1) Headache

1. I have a headache. (*ache = dull persistent pain*)
2. I have a hangover.
   (*hangover = a headache caused by too much alcohol*)
3. I have a pounding headache.
4. My head aches.
5. I feel dizzy. (*dizzy = lightheaded*)

(2) Stomach Problems

6. I have a stomachache.
7. My stomach is upset. (*upset = a slight stomach illness*)
8. I feel nauseated.
9. I feel like throwing up. (*throw up = vomit*)
10. I want to barf. (*barf = vomit*)

(3) Throat

11. I have a sore throat. (*sore = painfully sensitive; tender*)
12. My throat is red.
13. My voice is hoarse.

(4) Backache

14. I have a backache.
15. I have lower back pain.
16. I injured my spine.

(5) Cold and Flu

17. I feel a little under the weather.
18. I have a cold.
19. I think I'm catching the flu.
20. I have a touch of the flu. (*a touch of* = *a little*)
21. I don't feel very well today.
22. I feel a chill. (*i.e. I feel cold.*)
23. I have a fever.

(6) Fractures and Sprains

24. I fractured my leg.
25. I broke my arm.
26. I sprained my ankle.
27. You have a spiral fracture.
28. I have a compound fracture in my leg.
29. I twisted my elbow.
30. I turned my knee.

(7) Aches and Pains

31. My knee is sore.
32. I have a slight pain in my elbow.
33. My hand hurts. (*hurt* = *feel pain* ; *suffer*)
34. I have this terrible pain.

(8) Examinations

35. My thumb is swollen.
36. I hurt myself.
37. I wish to be diagnosed.
38. Would you please have a look at it?
39. I want a full physical examination.
40. Please examine this.
41. Please check my pulse.

(9) X-rays

42. I would like to X-ray your arm.
43. What is the result of my X-ray ?
44. The X-ray shows that you have a fracture.
45. The X-ray shows no sign of damage.
46. I want to take a picture of your bones.
47. I would like to do a CAT scan.
    (*CAT = computerized axial tomography*)

(10) Hospital Admission

48. I want to admit you to the hospital.
49. I think you should be admitted.

(11) Casts and Splints

50. I have to wear this cast for six weeks.
51. He's in a body cast.
52. I will be on crutches（拐杖）for a while.
53. I will be in plaster（石膏）for only one more week.
54. I have my knee wrapped in an Ace bandage.
55. I must keep this immobilized for a day or so.
56. I will put a splint on your finger.
57. The doctor told me to keep this splint on for a while.

(12) Medicine

58. Please have this prescription filled.
59. Take one every two hours.
60. You should take this after meals.
61. Apply this to the infected area every morning.
62. Put two drops in each eye.

LESSON 13

Vocabulary

Here are some typical terms that you should know.

(1) <u>Medicine</u>

1. aspirin 〔'æspərɪn〕
2. antibiotic 〔,æntɪbaɪ'atɪk〕
3. pain killer
4. penicillin 〔,penɪ'sɪlɪn〕
5. sleeping pill
6. vaccine 〔'væksɪn〕
7. vitamin
8. prescription drugs
   非經醫師處方不得買賣的藥品
9. iodine tincture 碘酒
10. cough drop 止咳藥片
11. eye drops
12. cough syrup 止咳糖漿

13. pill
14. tablet 〔'tæblɪt〕
15. capsule 〔'kæpsl〕
16. time-release 藥效持續的時間
17. drops
18. caplet 〔'kæplɪt〕

(2) <u>Hospital</u>

1. general hospital 綜合醫院
2. mental hospital 精神病院
3. medical center
4. nurse
5. doctor
   general practitioner 全科醫生
6. intern 〔'ɪntɜn〕
7. dermatology 〔,dɜmə'talədʒɪ〕
   dermatologist 〔,dɜmə'talədʒɪst〕
8. urology 〔jʊ'ralədʒɪ〕
   urologist 〔jʊ'ralədʒɪst〕

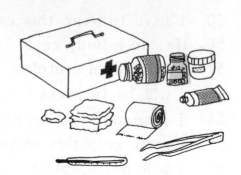

9. pediatrics 〔,pidɪ'ætrɪks〕
   pediatrician 〔,pidɪə'trɪʃən〕
10. neurology 〔njʊ'ralədʒɪ〕
    neurologist 〔njʊ'ralədʒɪst〕
11. psychiatry 〔saɪ'kaɪətrɪ〕
    psychiatrist 〔saɪ'kaɪətrɪst〕
12. surgery 〔'sɜdʒərɪ〕
    surgeon 〔'sɜdʒən〕
13. ear, nose, and throat
    specialist 耳鼻喉科醫生

(3) Medical Examinations

1. be allergic to 對～過敏
2. anemic〔əˈnɛmɪk〕
3. bleeding
4. blister〔ˈblɪstə〕
5. high blood pressure 高血壓
6. breathe in / out 吸／呼
7. burn
8. cramp〔kræmp〕
9. cure
10. diagnose〔ˌdaɪəgˈnos, -ˈnoz〕
11. dizziness
12. hemorrhage〔ˈhɛmərɪdʒ〕
13. inflammation〔ˌɪnfləˈmeʃən〕
14. injection〔ɪnˈdʒɛkʃən〕
    shot〔ʃɑt〕
15. itch
16. palpitate〔ˈpælpəˌtet〕
    heart palpitations 急促的心跳

(4) Names of Diseases

1. abscess〔ˈæbˌsɛs, -sɪs〕
2. apoplexy〔ˈæpəˌplɛksɪ〕
3. appendicitis〔əˌpɛndəˈsaɪtɪs〕
4. asthma〔ˈæsmə, ˈæzmə〕
5. athlete's foot 香港腳
   (Hong Kong Foot)
6. bronchitis〔brɑnˈkaɪtɪs〕

7. bruise〔bruz〕
8. Caesarean operation
   帝王式切開術
   C-section 剖腹產
9. cancer
10. chicken pox 水痘
11. cholera〔ˈkɑlərə〕

(be allergic to)

12. constipation〔ˌkɑnstəˈpeʃən〕
13. diabetes〔ˌdaɪəˈbitɪs, -tiz〕
14. diarrhea〔ˌdaɪəˈriə〕
15. heart attack
16. mental disease 精神病
17. pneumonia〔njuˈmonjə〕
18. polio〔ˈpolɪo, ˈpɑlɪo〕
19. pollution disease
    污染所引發之疾病
20. pregnancy〔ˈprɛgnənsɪ〕
21. seasickness〔ˈsiˌsɪknɪs〕
22. sneeze
23. tuberculosis〔tjuˌbɝkjəˈlosɪs〕
    (TB)
24. venereal disease 性病
    (VD)
25. virus〔ˈvaɪrəs〕

LESSON 13

Exercise **1**

Here are some short dialogues. For each question choose the correct answer.

1. A: How are you feeling today?
   B: _____ .
   (a) I broke my arm.
   (b) The doctor felt my condition was good.
   (c) I'm a little under the weather.
   (d) I felt it was a little strange.

2. A: What's the matter with you?
   B: _____ .
   (a) My operation isn't until next week.
   (b) I have a touch of the flu.
   (c) It hurts her right here.   (d) He sprained his back.

3. A: My cold won't yield to treatment.
   B: _____ .
   (a) Your medicine did not agree with me.
   (b) The doctor felt my pulse.
   (c) Try this medication, then.
   (d) I have a terrible headache, too.

4. A: I want to admit you to the hospital.
   B: _____ .
   (a) Since when have you been feeling like that?
   (b) How long will I be in?
   (c) You will be up and about in a few days.
   (d) My gums are sore.

5. A: What is the result of the X-rays?
   B: _____ .
   (a) Do you want to take more?
   (b) It shows you have a cold.
   (c) This may make you dizzy.
   (d) It's difficult to tell. We'll need more tests.

LESSON 13

Exercise 2

Answer the questions using the words in parentheses.

1. You don't look very well.
   (*headache*) _____

2. Where does it hurt?
   (*lower back*) _____

3. What's wrong?
   (*flu*) _____

4. How did you hurt yourself?
   (*baseball*) _____

5. Doctor, my leg really hurts.
   (*X-ray*) _____

6. How long has she been in the hospital?
   (*over a week*) _____

7. What did the doctor give him?
   (*prescription*) _____

8. What was the result of the X-ray?
   (*shows a fracture*) _____

9. Did you sprain your knee?
   (*broken*) _____

10. Has your cold cleared up yet?
    (*feel great*) _____

Lesson 14   A Job Interview

Be a success.
Get the job you want using English.

🎧 (A) LET'S TALK

A : What was your major in college, Miss Adams?

B : I took French.

A : Really? It's a very useful language to know especially in the travel industry. And now tell me why you're interested in this job?

B : For one thing, I thought I could use my French, and I'm very interested in the tourist industry.

A : Good. Now, is there anything else you'd like to know about the job?

B : Yes, first I was wondering what kind of training program you have for the new staff?

A : Sure, we have a two week orientation program for new staff.

B : And what would the salary and benefits be, please?

A : The salary range is $13,000 to 19,000. Here's a copy of our benefits package. Does that cover everything?

B : Yes, thank you.

A : Fine, I have your resume, and we'll be in touch with you as soon as we have reached a decision.

B : Thank you again. I hope to hear from you soon.

LESSON 14

Here are some typical interview situations.
Practice them with a partner.

🎧 (B) LET'S USE

LESSON 14

🎧 (C) LET'S PRACTICE

Here are some expressions you should know.

(1) Questions You'll Face

1. What are your qualifications? (*e.g. past jobs, school, etc...*)

2. Have you had business experience? (*i.e. experience in business*)

3. Do you have any recommendations?

4. Are you familiar with business correspondence?
   (***correspondence*** = *writing letters*)

5. Tell me something about your background and working experience.

6. Can you operate a computer?

7. How long have you been doing secretarial work?

8. What salary would be acceptable to you?

9. How soon can you start if we offer you a job?

10. Do you have any questions about the job?

11. What interested you especially in this position?

(2) About Yourself

12. I just completed a course in computer programming at a vocational institute in Taipei.

13. I studied French at a language institute for two years.

14. I can speak four languages.

15. I've been a secretary for five years in three different firms. (***firm*** = *company*)

16. I've been doing this kind of work ever since I graduated from college.

17. I graduated from college three years ago, and then I got a job at the computer center on Hsin Yi Road.

18. I think my previous experience and education makes me qualified for this job.

19. I like people and I like to travel.

20. I'd also like to learn more about air travel.

21. It seems to me that coordinating promotions gives you a chance to be creative.

(3) Why You Are Looking for a New Job

22. You're working as a government employee, aren't you?

23. I used to, but I quit last year and became a company employee.

24. Why did you quit the previous company?

25. I quit because of the salary.

26. It's a small company and there's not really much opportunity for promotion.

(4) Questions about the Job

27. I was wondering if it was a large sales office?

28. I'd like to know what kind of training program you have for the new staff.

29. When would the job start?

30. What would the salary and benefits be, please?

LESSON 14

🎧 (D) LET'S PLAY

Role play. Find a partner and take turns interviewing for each of the jobs below.

(1)   **EXHIBIT DESIGNER**

Big department store. Artistic, creative and work well alone. Some evenings and weekends.

(2)   **NURSE'S AIDE**

Nursing home. Like working with older people. Days or nights.

(3)   **WAITER / WAITRESS**

Friendly and efficient. Experience not necessary. Can work days, evenings or weekends.

(4)   **CAR MECHANIC**

2 years' experience. Know Japanese cars. Excellent salary. Full time/part time.

(5)   **PERSONNEL RECEPTIONIST**

Hardworking and efficient. Will train. Experience working with people.

(6)   **TRUCK DRIVER**

Long-distance. Full-time. Good driving record. Mechanical experience a plus.

LESSON 14

🎤 (E) LET'S READ

Read the application letter and circle the correct phrases.

45-3 Alley 25, Lane 89,
Hoping E. Rd., Sec. 3,
Taipei, Taiwan 10660
R.O.C.

Ms. Ellen Robertson
July 18, 1989
Personnel Manager
China Airlines
26. Nanking E. Rd., Sec. 3,
Taipei, Taiwan 10411
R.O.C.

Dear Ms. Robertson:

   I am writing about the newspaper ad for flight attendants.
   I am now a telephone operator for the Grand Hotel. I am good at languages--I speak French, English, German, and a little Spanish. I like to work with people and I also like to travel.
   I would like to make an appointment for an interview. I am enclosing my resumé.

                    Sincerely,

                    Liz Davis

● **Circle the letter of the correct phrase.**

1. Liz wants to
   a. study French.
   b. be a flight attendant.
   c. be a telephone operator.

2. She saw the ad
   a. in the China Post
   b. at the Grand Hotel
   c. at China Airlines.

3. Ms. Robertson works for
   a. the China Post.
   b. the Grand Hotel.
   c. China Airlines.

4. Liz likes to
   a. send her resume.
   b. travel.
   c. be a flight attendant.

LESSON 14

Exercise 1

In this exercise pretend that you are at a job interview. Answer the questions using your imagination.

1. I'd like to start by asking you some questions.
   First, where did you go to college?

   _____.

2. OK, and when did you get that degree?

   _____.

3. Can you tell me what made you apply for this job?

   _____.

4. Did you have a job before or is this your first?

   _____.

5. So you're looking for a change, then?

   _____.

6. And what do you actually know about advertising and advertising agencies?

   _____.

7. Do you like team work or do you prefer to work individually?

   _____ as part of a team.

8. What kind of salary do you expect for this job?

   Well, _____.

9. Do you have any questions about the company?

   Yes, _____.

LESSON 14

Exercise 2

Pretend you are applying for a job and fill out this application.

EMPLOYMENT APPLICATION
TERA ELECTRIC COMPANY

Print or type all answers.

Name	Date of Birth
Last First Middle	

Address	Telephone
Number Street	

	Date Available for Work
City Zip Code	

Do you have any health problems? ☐ yes
(if yes, please explain)   ☐ no

Have you or a relative ever worked for this
      company?   ☐ yes
      ☐ no

What position are you applying for?

Education

School	City	Dates Attended

Work Experience

Employer	City	Position	Date of Employment

All information on this form is true and complete to the best of my knowledge.

Signature	Date

||||||||||||| ● 學習出版公司門市部 ● |||||||||||||||

台北地區：台北市許昌街 10 號 2 樓 TEL：(02)2331-4060・2331-9209
台中地區：台中市綠川東街 32 號 8 樓 23 室
TEL：(04)2223-2838

||||||||||||||||||||||||||||||||||||||||||||||||||||

American Talks ②

編　　著／陳怡平
發 行 所／學習出版有限公司　　　☎ (02) 2704-5525
郵 撥 帳 號／0512727-2 學習出版社帳戶
登 記 證／局版台業 2179 號
印 刷 所／裕強彩色印刷有限公司
台 北 門 市／台北市許昌街 10 號 2 F　　☎ (02) 2331-4060・2331-9209
台 中 門 市／台中市綠川東街 32 號 8 F 23 室　　☎ (04) 2223-2838
台灣總經銷／紅螞蟻圖書有限公司　　☎ (02) 2799-9490・2657-0132
美國總經銷／Evergreen Book Store　　☎ (818) 2813622

售價：新台幣一百八十元正
2001 年 9 月 1 日一版四刷

ISBN 957-519-247-8

第二冊學習內容一覽表

LESSON	CONVERSATION	DIALOGUES	TYPICAL PHRASES	MOPE PRACTICE	EXERCISE
1	Making Plans	有關約人會面的對話。	練習詢問和決定見面的時間與地點的實況例句。	利用角色扮演的活動，練習計畫一次外出用餐。	Chart Study & Answer Questions
2	The Seasons	學習月份、日期及星期的說法。	練習有關季節天候變化的語句。	歌曲：The Months of the Year	測驗日期月份的寫法。
3	At the Hotel	練習看英文廣告，選擇喜歡的飯店投宿。	有關住宿飯店的各種實用語句，包括辦理住宿、退宿手續、客房服務等。	① 看圖造句 ② 常用字彙	Dialogue Reading
4	Emotional Expressions	各種情緒反應的實況對話。	練習喜怒哀樂各種情緒的表達法。	練習看圖說出情緒反應。	① Fill in the Blanks ② Complete the Dialogues
5	McDonald's Hamburger	在速食店中點餐的實況對話。	各種在速食店中用餐的例句。	① 角色扮演：在麥當勞點餐 ② 閱讀：McDonald's USA & McDonald's Taiwan	Multiple Choice
6	The Beauty Parlor	到美容院常用的實況對話練習	練習用英語與美容師溝通，說出想剪的髮型。	① 各種女士髮型名稱及美髮用具 ② 常用字彙	角色扮演
7	Getting a Haircut	到理髮院常用的實況對話練習。	練習用英語與理髮師溝通，說出想剪的髮型。	① 各種男士髮型名稱及用具 ② 常用字彙	角色扮演
8	The Post Office	角色扮演：練習在郵局的簡單對話句型。	到郵局寄信、寄包裹、買郵票、信封等實用語句	① 紙上遊戲：誰的記憶力好？ ② 常用字彙	Complete the Dialogues
9	The Department Store	認識百貨公司各部門的說法，及相關位置的表達。	在百貨公司購物所用到的實用例句。	① 閱讀：Department Stores in USA & Department Stores in Taiwan ② 常用字彙	角色扮演
10	An Evening at the Theater	到劇院觀賞歌劇表演的對話。	各種有關到劇院觀賞表演的實用語句，如購票、尋找座位、談論表演等等。	① 認識劇院的設備 ② 閱讀：Peking Opera	Complete the Dialogues
11	The World of Sports	認識各項運動的說法及句型練習。	有關於談論各項運動的實用例句。	閱讀：The Olympic Games	Match（配合題）
12	Public Transportation	認識各種海陸運輸工具。	練習搭公車、地下鐵、乘坐火車時的例句。	句型練習	Chart Study & Answer Questions
13	A Visit to the Doctor	練習各種病痛的說法。	包括向醫生描述各種疾病的說法如：感冒、牙、頭痛、胃痛、骨折等。	有關醫療的各種字彙	① Multiple Choice ② Complete Dialogues
14	A Job Interview	面試實況對話。	有關求職面試的問與答。	① 角色扮演：應徵工作 ② 閱讀：求職信函	① Complete the Dialogues ② 填寫一張英文履歷表

中外節日一覽表

中國節日

❖ 國曆節日

中華民國開國紀念日　Founding Anniversary
of the Republic of China ················· 1月1日

陽曆年　Solar（western）New Year ······ 1月1日

自由日　Liberty Day ·························· 1月23日

植樹節　Arbor Day ························· 3月12日

國父逝世紀念日　Memorial Day of
Dr. Sun Yat-sen's Death ················· 3月12日

青年節　Youth Day ························· 3月29日

兒童節　Children's Day ····················· 4月4日

蔣公逝世紀念日　Memorial Day of
President Chiang Kai-shek's Death ····· 4月5日

清明節　Tomb Sweeping Day ··············· 4月5日

勞動節　Labor Day ························· 5月1日

文藝節　Literary Day ······················· 5月4日

禁煙節　Opium Suppression Movement
Day ··· 6月3日

父親節　Father's Day ······················· 8月8日

記者節　Reporters' Day ····················· 9月1日

軍人節　Armed Forces Day ················· 9月3日

教師節　Teacher's Day（Confucius
Birthday）··································· 9月28日

雙十節　Double-Tenth Day ·········· 10月10日

光復節　Taiwan Restoration Day ······ 10月25日

蔣公誕辰紀念日　The Late President
Chiang Kai-shek's Birthday ········· 10月31日

國父誕辰紀念日　Dr. Sun Yat-sen's
Birthday ·································· 11月12日

行憲紀念日　Constitution Day ········· 12月25日

❖ 農曆節日

春節　Spring Festival ····················· 正月初一

陰曆年　Lunar New Year ················· 正月1日

農民節　Farmer's Day ····················· 正月8日

元宵節　Lantern Festival ················· 正月15日

端午節　Dragon Boat Festival ··········· 5月5日

中元節　Ghost Festival ···················· 7月15日

中秋節　Mid-Autumn（moon）
Festival ····································· 8月15日

重陽節　Double Ninth Festival ··········· 9月9日

西洋節日

主顯節　Epiphany〔ɪˈpɪfənɪ〕············· 1月6日

聖燈節　Candlemas〔ˈkændḷməs〕······ 2月2日

林肯誕辰　Lincoln's Birthday ········· 2月12日

情人（范倫泰）節　（St.）Valentine's
Day ··· 2月14日

婦女節　Women's Day ····················· 3月8日

復活節　Easter Sunday ···················· 3月21日

愚人節　April Fool's Day ·················· 4月1日

植樹節　Arbor Day ············· 4月5月的某一天

母親節　Mother's Day ········· 5月第2個禮拜天

美紀念陣亡將士日　Memorial Day ······ 5月30日

美國父親節　Father's Day ··············· 6月15日

美獨立紀念日　Independence Day ······· 7月4日

勞工節　Labor Day ············· 9月之第一個星期一

美國哥倫布紀念日　Columbus
Day ··· 10月12日

美國萬聖節前夕　Halloween ··········· 10月31日

萬聖節　All Saints' Day；
All Hallows Day ························· 11月1日

感恩節　Thanksgiving（Day）
························· 11月第4個星期四

聖誕節　Christmas ······················· 12月25日

常 用 諺 語

1. Absence makes the heart grow fonder.
   小別勝新婚；離別更增思念之情。

2. Actions speak louder than words.
   行動勝於言辭。

3. All work and no play makes Jack a dull boy.
   只是工作而不遊戲，會使人變得遲鈍。

4. As you sow, so shall you reap.
   種瓜得瓜；種豆得豆。

5. Beauty is in the eye of the beholder.
   情人眼裡出西施。

6. A bird in the hand is worth two in the bush.
   二鳥在林不如一鳥在手。

7. Birds of a feather flock together.
   物以類聚。

8. Blood is thicker than water.
   血濃於水。

9. When in Rome, do as the Romans do.
   入境隨俗。

10. Better be sure than sorry.
    安全總比後悔好，寧安勿躁。

11. Do not cast pearls before swine.
    勿對牛彈琴。

12. Don't count your chickens before they are hatched.
    不要打如意算盤。

13. Don't change horses in mid-stream.
    臨陣莫換將。

14. Don't make a mountain out of a molehill.
    不要小題大作。

15. Don't put all your eggs into one basket.
    勿孤注一擲。

16. Don't put the cart before the horse.
    勿本末倒置。

17. The early bird catches the worm.
    早起的鳥兒有蟲吃。

18. An eye for an eye, and a tooth for a tooth.
    以牙還牙，以眼還眼。

19. Fine feathers make fine birds.
    人要衣裝，佛要金裝。

20. First come, first served.
    捷足先登。

21. A fool and his money are soon parted.
    愚人難聚財。

22. God helps those who help themselves.
    天助自助者。

23. A friend in need is a friend indeed.
    患難見眞情。

24. Haste makes waste.
    欲速則不達。

25. Good company on the road is the shortest cut.
    良伴同行路途短。

26. Half a loaf is better than none.
    聊勝於無。

27. Health is better than wealth.
    健康勝於財富。

28. Honesty is the best policy.
    誠實是最上策。

29. It is better to give than to take.
    施比受更有福。

30. It never rains but it pours.
    屋漏偏逢連夜雨；禍不單行。

31. It's no use crying over spilled milk.
    覆水難收。

32. It is never too late to mend.
    亡羊補牢；猶未晚矣。

33. Jack of all trades, master of none.
    萬能先生，樣樣通；樣樣鬆。

34. A little knowledge is a dangerous thing.
    一知半解最危險。

35. Necessity is the mother of invention.
    需要爲發明之母。

36. Make hay while the sun shines.
    把握時機。

37. Like father, like son.
    有其父必有其子。

38. Learn to walk before you run.
    學跑之前先學走。

39. Knowledge is power.
    知識就是力量。

40. A rolling stone gathers no moss.
    滾石不生苔，轉業不聚財。

41. Man proposes, God disposes.
    謀事在人，成事在天。

42. A stitch in time saves nine.
    及時的一針補九針。

43. Time and tide wait for no man.
    歲月不待人。

44. Time is money.
    時間就是金錢。

45. Too many cooks spoil the broth.
    人多厨子壞了一鍋粥。

46. Where there's a will there's a way.
    有志者事竟成。

47. Easier said than done.
    說來容易做來難。

48. The more you have, the more you want.
    擁有越多，想要越多。

49. Never judge by appearances.
    勿以貌取人。

50. Never put off till tomorrow what may be done today.
    今日事，今日畢。

Australia

New Zealan